Neverland

GENRE: YA/FANTASY

This book is a work of fiction. Names, places, characters and incidents are either the product of the author's imagination or are used fictitiously. Any resemblance to actual people, living or dead, businesses, organizations, events or locales is entirely coincidental.

NEVERLAND
Copyright © 2014 by Anna Katmore
Cover design by Laura J Miller, www.anauthorsart.com
Edited by Annie Cosby, www.AnnieCosby.com
All cover art copyright © 2014 by Anna Katmore

ANNA KATMORE

ALSO BY ANNA KATMORE

play with me

Some time before I started writing this book, I asked my readers to lend me their names for some of the characters. It was totally amazing how many of them answered to that post. Unfortunately, there aren't as many characters in this book as I got beautiful names and the choice was incredibly hard.

Here's who made it into the book...

Angelina McFarland
(Angel, the heroine)

Brittney Renae Goff
(The fairy bug, one of the twins)

Paulina
(The honey bunny, one of the twins)

Tameeka Taylor
(Tami, the pixie)

Remona Karim and Karima Olayshia Bre'Shun
(The fairy sisters)

Thank you for naming my characters!

ANNA KATMORE

Neverland

A novel by

ANNA KATMORE

Chapter 1

A laughing bundle of strawberry blond hair squirms on my bed. "Angel! Angel, stop! I'm gonna pee my pants!"

Immediately, I stop tickling my baby sister, sit down on the bedside, and put her on my lap, giving her one of those *you-do-that-and-I-rip-off-your-stuffed-bunny's-head* looks. She knows I would never really do it, but the threat works every time.

At that moment, the exact likeness of the five-year-old on my legs comes walking through my door. Only this one's wrapped in her purple fairy dress that has a pair of net wings attached at the back. The chiffon buckles angrily, and I wonder if she's been sitting on the floor with her dolls for the past half hour.

She waves her glowing pink fairy wand that has a star tip in my face. "Why is Paulina screaming like the Barbie Dreamhouse is burning down again?"

The Barbie Dreamhouse didn't burn down...completely. It caught fire when we lit some candles on Christmas Eve a few weeks ago. Dad draped a blanket—Mom's favorite cashmere quilt—over the wooden house and extinguished the flames. The house was saved, but its west wing needed reconstruction and my sisters bugged me to paint the sitting room walls candy pink to cover the smoke marks.

"She's screaming because the ugly Captain Hook is on the hunt for little princesses again," I snarl, before putting Paulina back on my bed and chasing after a squeaking Brittney Renae, who makes a dash for the hallway and, in her polished, dark-red, patent-leather shoes, runs for her life.

I catch her right before she makes it to our parents' bedroom and would have slammed the door in my face, no doubt. With one arm around her tiny body, I scoop her up and flop with her onto the king-size bed that will stay empty once again tonight because our parents are at another charity thing, which they do almost every weekend. I claw my index finger like it's the ruthless pirate's silver hook. "I'm the captain of the pirates, and I'll slice you with my hook from your belly to your nose," I say in a deep, rumbling voice.

Brittney Renae buries her face against my shoulder and giggles. She bursts into laughter like a volcano exploding as soon as I dig my fingers between her ribs.

There's nothing in this world that delights me more than the sound of the twins' laughs. Their carefree temperament catches me every time, whether I'm stuck in the middle of studies for my high school graduation in just a few months, or helping Miss Lynda with the household.

Mom and Dad don't like me giving our stone-aged housekeeper a hand in the kitchen. *Girls from a good family don't get their hands dirty* is what they taught me all my life. I wasn't allowed to play in the mud with other kids, nor could I wear torn jeans with hoodies, or listen to rock music in my room without headphones on.

When the twins' nanny moved away last spring and my parents couldn't find a replacement that did an equally good job, my chance for a change had come. I offered to watch the girls on weekends, if my parents would allow me to wear normal clothes instead of the expected blouses, pantsuits or classy dresses—at least inside the house and as long as we weren't expecting any guests for a dinner banquet. I hate being dressed like one of the Queen's closest confidants.

Mom agreed after a long discussion dominated by sighs. Dad insisted they keep looking for a new nanny, but when the twins made their huge puppy eyes at him, he gave in. No one in this family can resist Paulina's or Brittney Renae's soulful looks when they push the pretty-please button.

Dad's condition to let me wear my own choice of

clothes inside was that I meet Jasper Allensik, the son of his business partner, who apparently was related to the royals in some convoluted way. I agreed but later nailed Dad down on the fact that the deal was: I only had to date the guy if I liked him at least sixty-five percent. Which I did not.

Jasper Allensik is a jerk. He's tall, thin, wears his oiled black hair in a side part and drinks tomato juice at every meal he eats, which again comes out through his nose if something absolutely not-funny makes him laugh, like a ridiculous article in the *Financial Times*.

After a long school day in London, I like drinking strawberry milk with my fries if I have a chance to drop in at Burger King, but I never release the milk through my nose, laughing or not.

We usually don't have strawberry milk at home, because Dad isn't a big fan of that, and neither do we get to eat fries. Miss Lynda is advised to serve things like lobster, chicken breast, and sometimes even caviar on toast. Brittney Renae and Paulina are allowed to skip the fish-egg antipasti, but from the time I turned twelve, I was told to get used to the god-awful stuff, so I wouldn't embarrass my parents again by spitting a mouthful back into the bowl in front of their guests. Yeah, sometimes it's just exhausting to be the firstborn in George McFarland's house.

I grab Brittney Renae by her waist and set her on her

feet. "Now you have to make their bed again," she says, waving her wand at me.

I obey. Miss Lynda makes the twins' beds at least five times a day to keep my parents pleased, since they are sticklers for tidiness. I make my own bed every morning and try to keep it that way until the evening, which doesn't happen often so I remake it as often as Miss Lynda does the twins' beds. But to frolic with my sisters in my parents' bed is a sacrosanct no-no. We aren't even allowed in this room. But George and Mary are out, so who would stop us from turning the mansion into a playground?

I pull at the sheets' ends and smooth them with my palms until they are perfectly straight again. The little fairy bug has left me alone and probably went back to her room to continue playing tea party with her dolls. As soon as I turn off the light in the room and step out into the wide carpeted hallway, Paulina skips into my arms. I lift her up and wonder why she's grinning like a birthday clown. It usually means she has a brilliant idea...or that Miss Lynda smuggled some homemade cookies into the McFarland house, which happened just this afternoon.

"What is it, honey bunny?" I ask and rake my fingers through her long, straight hair that's thick like weeds.

"I have a surprise for you."

Uh oh. Her last surprise gave me a strand of green hair. Thank goodness finger paint isn't a permanent dye. I shroud my grimace with a fake smile. "Great! Let's see it."

"It's a tattoo."

"Bloody hell!"

Paulina instantly covers her mouth with her tiny hands and sucks in a shocked breath, but I don't care. My parents aren't here to send me to my room for swearing. In a slight panic, I put my sister down, squat in front of her, and shove up the sleeves of her red panda-bear sweater, one at a time, checking her arms for images of any kind.

She giggles. "Not me, silly."

Phew! My mother would have killed me.

"It's your name, so you have to put it on," Paulina informs me, and my chin knocks against my chest.

"What?"

She holds out her hand und uncurls her fist. In her palm lies a paper snippet with the word *Angel* on it. No one but the twins call me that, and it's the only word in the world they can spell yet. On their demand, I had to teach them—over an entire week. If it wasn't for the cute reason that they couldn't say Angelina properly when they learned to speak, it would have been totally ridiculous that I was called Angel. Seriously, I look like anything but. I didn't inherit Mom's angelic strawberry blond locks but instead Dad's raven black hair, which I wear nowadays in a chin-length bob. My skin is pale and my dark brown eyes stand out from the rest of my face.

I take the cutout from my sister's hand and examine

it. It's one of those tattoos you find in Disney princess magazines. The letters are curvy and purple with a mist of small stars underneath. Fantastic. And she wants me to put that where? On my forehead so my parents can blow a gasket about it in the morning?

As if she can read my mind, Paulina shrugs. "We can put that on the inside of your forearm. You always wear those black sweaters. Mommy won't see it."

Who could ever say no to a hopeful heart-shaped face like that? I blow out a resigned breath and make a mental note to scrub the tattoo off tomorrow morning before joining my family downstairs for breakfast. "All right. Let's do it."

I usher her across the hallway into the bathroom. The light comes on as soon as we open the door and reflects in the shiny peach and white tiles all over the place. I sit down on the edge of the oval white tub and watch the busy dwarf pull out the stool from under the washbasin so she can step on it and reach the faucet. She then brings a wet cloth and tampers with my arm while I patiently wait.

When she's done and radiantly happy, the fairy bug appears in the doorway. "What are you two doing in here?" she asks and stems her little fists on her hips. For once, she didn't bring her wand.

"I tattooed Angel's name on her forearm," Paulina informs her.

"Really?" Brittney Renae dances over to us, clapping her hands when she sees the result. "Aw, this is so beautiful! You must never wash your arm again and leave this on forever."

"Why? So I can use my forearm as a cheat sheet in case I forget my name?"

Paulina scrunches up her face. "What's a *jeet jeet*?"

"It's something you have in...ah, never mind." Better to change the topic and save myself from being dragged into another what-and-why inquisition that always leave me with a headache. Downstairs, the tall grandfather clock starts chiming eight. "Time for bed, girls."

The twins smile, because getting ready for bed starts in the same way whenever we're alone at home. Everybody finds a spot in Paulina's bed, Brittney Renae brings a book, and I read. We do this before all the other stuff, like brushing their teeth and changing into their flannel PJ's, because Brittney Renae likes to keep her costume on until the very last minute.

I sprawl out on the bed, leaning against the headboard, let my sisters snuggle up to me at either side, and open the book that Brittney Renae hands me. It's *Peter Pan*. I'm not surprised. It's their favorite, and I read this book to them night after night. The twins speak every single line with me while I read.

With the girls pressed to my sides, I soon get warm in the heated room. I pull my sweater over my head and toss it at the end of the bed then continue reading.

"The pirate took the kids aboard his mighty ship, the Jolly Roger," all three of us say with the same dramatic edge to our voices. *"He tied them to the mast in the middle and laughed into their frightened faces. The dirty crew hurrahed their captain, each waving a flag in their hands. For they all knew, today was the day that Peter Pan would lose the battle."*

"Oh no," Paulina whines when I take a breath and turn the page. "What if the ugly Captain Hook catches him this time?"

I roll my eyes. She knows exactly how this tale goes. But every time we read it, she gets sucked into the story so much that her fears seem genuine and her tiny hands clench into shaking fists.

I let the girls look at the pictures for a while, before we reveal the ending together and everyone takes a relieved breath—including me. I don't know why I do it. Possibly because of the twins' infectious excitement whenever I read the story of Peter Pan.

I shut the book and put it back on Paulina's nightstand. We will surely read it again tomorrow night. The girls know what comes next and, without complaints, they both head into the bathroom to brush their teeth. While they're gone, I open the French doors that lead to a semicircle Victorian balcony. In the moonlight the slowly falling snowflakes look like a romantic rain of stars.

A cold breeze wafts around my body. Goosebumps rise on my bare arms and remind me that the French doors in my own room have been open for the past couple of hours. I shut the cold out from my sister's room and head back to mine. It's freezing cold in here, but before I close the French doors, I can't resist stepping out into the dancing flakes. I drag my feet through the thin layer of snow on the concrete balcony, leaving a trail with my tennis shoes.

My hands braced on the marble railing, I tilt my head skyward and catch some snowflakes with my mouth. The flakes melt away on my tongue and more keep falling on my face where they tangle with my lashes. It's that time of the year I like best. Everything is calm and peaceful outside. I look down at our wide English garden and imagine a deer coming out from behind the few trees at the very back. But nothing happens. We live just outside London. There's no city bustling around here, but we're still too far away from any woods to glimpse a deer or rabbit scurrying by.

"Angel!"

With my mouth still open and my tongue lolling out to catch more snow, I turn to the left and find the fairy bug out on Paulina's balcony. We're separated only by three meters of space and the crown of a common ash tree planted close to the house between our balconies. I straighten. "What's up?"

"You forgot your sweater." She holds out my black sweater in her tiny hands.

"Toss it over!" I walk to the left side of my balcony and stretch out my arms to catch the bundle of fabric. But her aim is as bad as my mother's taste in music, and the sweater lands in the top of the tree. "Ah no." I sigh and lean over the railing as far as I can, but there's no way I can grab the sweater. It's caught in the many twigs and branches.

It's only a few inches away, so I get a hold on the façade of the house and climb onto the broad marble balustrade. This way I'm able to lean farther out and finally reach one sleeve. My fingers around it, I want to step off the railing again, but it's slick from the snow, and I slip. A high-pitched cry bursts out of my throat as I struggle to catch my balance. I pray that somehow I'll come down on the inside of my balcony. But when I catch a glimpse of Brittney Renae's shocked face as I fall, I know this is going to hurt.

Chapter 2

I fall. A scream rips from me. The cold wind carries me in a spiral of fast-moving air. I open my eyes which for some reason I had kept shut until now. There's nothing around me. Really, nothing. I face a clear blue summer sky. Panic rises in my chest. I'm still falling—where in the world am I?

In my right fist, I hold the sleeve of a black sweater that flutters over my head like a helium-filled balloon. It does nothing to slow me down. Then I remember. *Jeez, the balcony!* I lost balance. I should have landed on the ground by now and broken each and every little bone in my body. So why the heck haven't I?

I turn and look down. Cotton candy clouds float beneath me. I can see my shadow on the fluffy white mass as I near them, and seconds later, I fall right through them.

ANNA KATMORE

My scream fades to a terrified whimper. As I emerge from the clouds, I finally see land beneath me. Luscious green hills, a thick jungle, and in the distance, colorful houses dotting an old seaport. The island I'm speeding toward is shaped like a half moon. There's nothing beneath to break my fall.

This is insane. People don't just fall right out of the sky. I pull the sweater to my chest and hug it tight with trembling arms. Oh God, I'm going to be mash in a minute.

I'm coming down too fast on the jungle. The Caribbean-blue water surrounding the island fades from my view. All there is below me are trees and bushes. A taller tree stands out from a little clearing and I miss the wide top by a few feet.

As I zoom past the top branches, I catch a glimpse of a face between the leaves. The person attached to it shoots forward and stops at the end of the longest branch. Holy cow, there's a boy in a grass-green tee and brown leather pants scaling the branches of the tree. He follows my fall with his surprised gaze, then he cups his hands around his mouth and shouts, "Watch out! It's raining girls today!"

It takes me a moment to realize he's not speaking to me, but to a group of boys on the ground. Boys that I'm going to squash in seconds. They all tilt their heads up and stare at me with stunned expressions. And then the weirdest thing happens. Out of nowhere, each of them pulls a black umbrella and they all stretch it, as though I could be fended off like rain.

ARE THEY NUTS?

Facing my end, I shriek the hell out of my lungs. But right before I land, something catches me and lifts me high in the air again. It's the guy in the green t-shirt who saves me. "Ugh, girl. You scream like a tortured pig. Mind stopping that?" he says, grimacing, and cuddles me tight against his chest as he freaking flies with me over the jungle.

My mouth wide open, I fall silent and gaze at his face. An instant later, my arms wrap around his neck in a death-hold.

He turns a sly grin at me. "Hi there."

I say nothing. I just can't believe it. This boy appears a little younger than I am, looks totally normal with blue eyes, thick brown hair and all, but he's sailing on the thermal wind like a kite. And I with him.

"Are you afraid of flying?" he asks me.

"I don't know," my croak comes out. I think that I'm usually not, but then I don't remember ever being carried across the sky like this.

"Well, if you are, you shouldn't be jumping off clouds, you know."

"I wasn't." A slippery balcony railing should have sealed my death. Then again...what if I was dead? And this was the other side? I pinch the boy's cheek and he yips.

Thank goodness he felt that. No dreaming and no waking up in heaven. A relieved sigh escapes through my clenched teeth.

The guy lands on his feet by his friends—all teenagers by the looks of them—with me still in his arms. Carefully, he releases first my legs and waits until I stand steadily on the grassy ground in the small clearing before he loosens his grip on me. He's a few inches taller than me and slim. Doesn't his mother feed him enough? But then he's probably not fully grown yet. Most boys around sixteen look a little underfed.

He holds out his hand. "I'm Peter. Peter Pan."

With some reluctance, I shake it. "I'm..." I begin, but that's all. For some strange reason, there's no information about myself stored in my mind. What the hell—?

He tilts his chin low and searches my face. "You forgot your own name?"

"Obviously," I admit, totally forlorn, scrunching up my face. "And what's worse, I have no idea why I just fell out of the sky."

"You don't know what you did in the clouds?" Peter demands.

"No. The last thing I remember is falling down the side of our house back in London. It's winter. Everything should be covered in..." Uncertain, I look around and add, "Snow."

"Where's London?" one of the boys whispers to

another. "And what's snow?"

"I don't know," says the other. "Maybe she lost her mind."

"Ooh, that's bad," the first one whispers back, loud enough for everybody to hear. "I bet Hook hit her with a cannonball."

I run my fingers through my hair and look down at myself. Everything seems just fine. I sure wasn't hit by a stupid cannonball.

"What's this?" Peter takes my hand once again and twists it so that the inside of my wrist is up. *"Angel,"* he reads out loud. "Maybe that's your name? Would make sense you have it tattooed on you, since you seem to forget it."

I examine the purple letters on my skin. Stars are brushed beneath the name. Is this real? It looks familiar but I don't remember when I had one done. Rubbing my thumb over the tattoo doesn't make it disappear. "Could be," I agree with Peter.

"Well then, nice to meet you, Angel!" he cheers and shakes my hand again as if we just met. "Welcome to Neverland."

"Neverland..." I test the sound of the word on my tongue. The name rings a bell. Somewhere far back in my mind. Too far for me to put a finger on. Whatever, I've always been a slouch in geography. Not so much in physics, though—I do know for a fact that humans shouldn't be able to fly. So the really nagging question is this: Is Neverland real, or am I just about to go gaga?

When Peter releases me, the boys grab my hand one after the other and rather enthusiastically introduce themselves. They all look between fourteen and sixteen years old, but they jump up and down like excited preschoolers.

"Hi, Angel, I'm Skippy!" one of them shouts in my face. He has amazingly big ears and huge round eyes. He reminds me a bit of an elf, though he has inclined teeth like a troll.

"I'm Sparky!" says the next, already taking my left hand before Skippy even lets go of my right.

"This is Toby, and I'm Stan!"

"How are you doing, Angel? I'm Loney."

"My name's Skippy!"

Yeah, we heard that before.

"I'm Toby!" ... "I'm Sparky!" ... "Skippy, that's me!"

More handshaking, and I'm getting a little dizzy. The guys pull on my arms and make me twist from one side to the other. They laugh and keep telling me their names as if each time was the first.

"Lost Boys, leave her alone!" Peter Pan shouts over the noise and I have my hands back to myself. I throw him a grateful look. He nods then steps forward and picks up the sweater that I dropped when they all got so excited about me. As he holds it up and glances at the front, his brows knit together. "Are you friends with Captain Hook?"

I mirror his expression. "Captain who?" Knowing his question has something to do with what he sees on my sweater, I reach for it, but Peter pulls it away quickly, then he pushes off the ground and levitates out of my reach. It's totally crazy to see this boy flying like a freaking balloon.

"Captain Hook," he repeats with a scolding growl and turns my sweater around so everybody sees the *Pirates of the Caribbean* image on the front. It's a skull with a bandana, and crossed torches burn behind it.

All the boys suck in a loud breath and jump one step back. Two for Skippy. "You sure you aren't one of his pirates?" he demands.

"Do I look like a pirate?" I snap back but quickly shut my mouth and inspect myself. *Do* I look like a pirate? I'm wearing the same clothes as a few minutes ago, when I was playing with the twins: blue jeans, a black tee and light grey tennis shoes. They don't seem like the right clothes for a pirate ship, but then who can say what's normal in this place, given there's a boy hovering two feet above me?

Peter tosses the sweater at me. "If you're one of his spies, you can tell your captain he'll never get the treasure! And sending girls is so beneath him."

"Hey!" I fold my arms over my chest. "I don't know any pirates! I live in an exclusive neighborhood just outside London. We have a huge, clean house, a cook and housekeeper, and every second Saturday of the month my parents give a dinner banquet for friends and business partners. No one skewers anybody with a saber there!"

"So you admit you do know about piracy custom then!" Peter accuses me. I roll my eyes in refusal of this unbelievable situation and rub my hands over my face. Slowly, Peter levitates up and down in front of me a few times, scratching his chin. "Fine. Let's say you aren't a pirate. What are we to do with you then?"

I let out a long breath and suggest with a surge of hope, "Help me get back home to England?"

Puckering his lips, he considers. "Okay. We can do that." Suddenly, his face lights up. "Tomorrow!"

"No, wait! I have to—" But it's too late. Peter somersaults in the air and comes down to reach under my arms, cutting me off. I have no chance to escape. He lifts me up again and flies with me to the top of the tree. I scream all the way. When he lands on a thick branch, he waggles his eyebrows. "Let me show you our home."

Home? I try to catch a glimpse around me to make out a house somewhere close, but apart from the thick jungle I can't see anything. And then Peter hustles me forward. "What the hell—" I drop down into the middle of the tree. Everything goes dark. It seems like I'm falling right through the trunk, which is outright crazy. What weird land is this?

I kamikaze-fall a few feet then feel the smooth surface of a slide at my back. It turns me in a new direction. Round and round in a spiral I go down, and if this wasn't the scariest moment since I fell through the clouds, it would actually be fun. The slide leads into the center of the tree that seems even bigger from the inside. On my mad descent, I scan the tree's interior with wide open eyes.

The trunk is completely carved out. Small windows are built into the bark, and pictures are hanging on the round-about wall. Cozy looking sleeping booths are hewn into the sides where big branches sprout from the trunk, and rope ladders lead down from each of them. This is amazing.

This is insane!

The slide ends abruptly and I'm catapulted into a trampoline. Lying spread-eagle, I breathe hard and wait until the wobbling of the net stops. Jeez, what a ride!

"Make way!" I barely had time to gather myself, when Peter's warning booms through the inside. A moment later, Loney, the boy with a fox-fur hat that still has ears, comes sliding down my way. Peter must have lifted him to the top of the tree like me.

Panicky, I crawl off the trampoline and wait until all the guys have come down, one by one. Peter is the last to follow. He, of course, doesn't climb out of the trampoline but simply glides down through the air right in front of me. Bowing deep, he sweeps his arm sideways. "Welcome to the Empire of Pan."

"Your empire consists of an entire tree?" I mock him.

"It does. But you haven't seen all of it yet." He wraps an arm around my shoulders and pulls me along with him. "Here's where we eat when we're lucky on the rabbit hunt."

The three seconds he grants me to look around the spacious area dominated by a huge, round wooden table with eight tree-trunk chops for chairs hardly seem enough to take in the full beauty of this place. We walk on to a spot right behind the trampoline that's plastered with mattresses. Lots of ropes and hammocks hang around.

Peter catches me unawares and pushes me forward. I land on my front on a pile of pillows and quickly roll on my back. "What did you do that for?"

Instead of an answer, he throws a sword at me. I cover my head with my arms in self-protection. The sword lands on my belly and pushes an *ugh* out of my lungs. It's carved from wood. Thank God, it's just a toy and not a medieval one made of iron.

"If you want to become one of us, you have to learn how to fight," he informs me with a glint in his eyes as he pulls another wooden saber from the belt around his waist and attacks me.

Like a rolled-over turtle, I try to defend myself from his blows, but each time his wooden toy hits mine, a nasty vibration rattles up my arm. I jump to my feet and parry his next blow. That was actually really good of me. I grin. But a second later, Peter somehow twists the sword out of my hand and it flies in a high arch across the room. He pushes me on my back again and places the tip of his saber to my throat. "Game over."

Toby catches my weapon and comes over. He pinches his nose closed and mocks me by imitating the sound of a pooping cow. Drops of his saliva spray down in a mist. "That was a pathetic attempt of becoming a Lost Boy, Angel."

"I don't intend to be one!" I climb to my feet and fight my way past Peter and the boy who's wearing his black hair in a ponytail with an undercut, and off the pillow and mattress nest.

Peter is at my side in a second again, taking my hand to drag me on. "Don't be sad. We'll practice with you every day, and soon you'll fit right in with us."

Practice? Fit right in? Didn't he just hear me? "I'm not going to live here, Peter. I told you that I have to find my way home." I pause. "And what was that about the *Lost Boys* anyway?"

"We can discuss this later. First, I want you to meet someone." He grins, the wooden sword still in his hand.

Even though there were so many windows on my ride down here, I notice that this place is unusually dark for daylight, but tinted in a soft glow. There are no

ANNA KATMORE

windows in this section, so I scan for the source of the light.

"Candles?" I burst out as I shoot around to face Peter. "Inside a tree?" Lanterns are placed everywhere. Our shadows are dancing on the wall, and for a tiny second I think Peter's shadow is mocking me by lifting its shoulders, even though Peter himself just looks at me with his hands in his pockets.

I'm getting a really bad feeling in here.

"Relax, Angel." Peter rolls his eyes. "We might not be grown-ups, but we're not stupid. We know how to handle fire. Anyway," he changes the subject and drags me past the mattress playground toward a small door. "This is Tameeka's room. Let's hope she's home."

Did he say room? But all this is much too big to fit into a tree. How's that possible? I stroke my palm across the wall next to the door. It's made of stone. And mud. Realization begins to dawn; we're no longer inside the tree. This place is built beneath it, into the earth. What a brilliant idea! Now it's clear why they need all the candles.

Peter knocks on the door and I stand back until it opens. A thin girl, maybe eight years old, pops her golden blond head out. As I see her sparkling green eyes and her pointed ears peaking through the locks, I gasp.

"Tami, meet Angel," Peter introduces us as Tameeka emerges from her room. "Angel fell out of the sky today."

Seeing her full feminine figure, I clap my hands over

my mouth. This is no normal child. She wears a short dress made of ivy leaves and there's a pair of see-through butterfly wings attached to her back. *Dear God, am I on some magic mushroom high?*

Tami comes forward, pirouettes on her bare toes and curtseys in front of me. "Nice to meet you, Angel." Her voice sounds like Christmas bells. "Did you get lost?"

"Well...yes," I murmur, shaking her tiny elfin hand. "How did you know?" But considering there's a house built into a tree, Peter can fly, and she's something closer to a fairy than a human child, I shouldn't wonder, really.

Tami tilts her head and smiles like I missed the obvious. "Everybody Peter brings here got lost somehow."

I turn to Peter Pan with quirked eye brows. "Really?" Then my gaze skates over the boys in the room.

They avoid my look, tuck their hands deep into their pockets, and poke their toes into the ground. All but Sparky. The stout boy just peels a banana and shoves it into his mouth, grinning and shrugging his shoulders. "Neverland is cool. None of us ever want to leave again," he tells me around the banana mush.

I face Peter. "You brought all the guys here to live with you?"

"Well—" He sounds defensive all of a sudden as he jumps backward up onto one of the hammocks, where he swings leisurely back and forth. "I gave them a home when they didn't know where to go. Toby and Stan were washed up on the shore one day, Skippy was hanging in a tree when I found him, and I had to save Sparky and Loney from the clutches of Captain Hook. It was their choice to stay."

There was that name again: Hook. Every time somebody mentions that name, the boys grimace. "Who is this captain that Sparky and Loney needed to be rescued from?" I want to know.

"Ooh, Hook is the ugliest, meanest and scariest man in Neverland," Stan tells me with a cruel look and clawed fingers. All the others agree with enthusiastic nods. "His face is scarred something awful, his nose is longer than a raven's beak, and there's a hook on his right arm." He pulls the zipper of his bear-fur vest closed, as if speaking about Hook gives him chills. "He's the worst pirate sailing these waters. His only aim is to steal our treasure, and he won't stop at anything to get it. He would let us all walk the plank with tied hands in a heartbeat."

"In fact, Peter had to save us more than once in the past," Skippy adds in a dead-serious tone. Then he presses his palms over Tameeka's ears and his voice drops to a whisper. "Hook never gets tired of making new plans to kidnap our little pixie and steal the map to the treasure's den."

Tami fends him off and scoffs in his face, standing on her tiptoes. "You don't have to do that all the time. I'm not a baby. I know what he's after."

Skippy placates her, holding his palms up. "Just trying to be sensitive."

"You? Sensitive? Hah!" Peter laughs and flies out of the hammock. He smacks Skippy over his head with the toy sword. "The sharks around the Jolly Roger are more sensitive than you."

Skippy takes on the challenge and runs to grab another wooden weapon from the mattress playground. The Lost Boys holler and cheer as Peter and Skippy fight a perfect battle where neither manages to touch the other with his sword.

I watch them in deep fascination, until someone tugs on my hand. Turning my head, I find Tami next to me. She sighs. "He does this every time."

"What? Start a fight?"

"No, they aren't really fighting." She laughs. "It's just a game. Peter doesn't like us being too serious."

"Is Peter a Lost Boy, too?" I wonder out loud.

"Oh no!" When she shakes her head, golden dust rains out of her hair. "He's the only one who came here for a reason. He never wanted to grow up. So he ran away."

Her words intrigue me, but more so does the raining gold. I catch some and rub it between my fingers. It disappears. "What's this?"

"Pixie dust. You've never heard of it?"

Should I have? I cock my head then shake it.

A slow grin spreads on her childish face. "With the right thought in mind, it can help you fly."

Fly. Like Peter? Damn if I didn't fall right into a fairy tale. "I'm afraid there's no such thing where I come from."

"Where *do* you come from?"

"A city in Great Britain. It's called London." Full of hope to get a reaction of recognition from her, I lift my brows.

"Ah, I see. London," she replies with a meaningful look. Anticipation kick-starts my heart. Then she puckers her lips. "Never heard that name before."

I grab my head between my palms and moan, frustration taking over. This can't be true. Someone here must know about my hometown. "Where do the Lost Boys come from?" I press then. "I mean, where did they live before they got washed up on the shores of this island?"

"The boys don't remember where they came from. Nobody knows." Tami's tone is matter-of-fact. "And it's better this way, too. I think if they did, they'd try to get back home."

"How can you say that? Of course they should try to go home. They surely have families who are missing them."

The little pixie shrugs. "Maybe they have, maybe they haven't. Anyway, it doesn't matter now. When they made the choice to live here, Neverland fully embraced them. They are part of it now. You heard Sparky before. No one wants to ever leave again." She smiles a warm, welcoming smile.

My heart sinks and I feel totally lost and alone. I don't want to become a part of Neverland. I want to go home to the twins and my parents. What will happen to Brittney Renae and Paulina without me? The fairy bug saw me fall. They'll run down and outside. What will they do when they realize I'm no longer there...in their world?

A shudder, cold as a scoop of ice cream, skitters down my spine. This is just too much to wrap my mind around. When I gaze at Tami once more, I remember what she said about Peter before. About his wish to never grow up. "How old is Peter?"

Tami's delicate butterfly wings start to flap. She takes off from the ground, flies a circle around me and lands on my other side, giggling. "How old does he look to you?"

I let my attention wander back to the battling boys and study Peter Pan's face for a moment. "Sixteen?"

Tami shakes her head and more pixie dust rains down. "He was fifteen when he left his home and came to live in the jungle. That was a very long time ago."

I rub my neck and come to the conclusion that nothing works right in Neverland. This is a seriously queer place. "And all the boys have been the same age for..."

"As long as they've been here," she finishes my sentence.

"Does this mean, if I stay, I'll be forever seventeen?"

"Yes."

Heck, I don't want to be stuck in the body of a teenager for eternity. I want to grow up. And what's with the guys not remembering where they come from? What if I too forget my family one day? Raking my hands over my skull, I drag in a scared breath. "Really, I can't stay here. I have to go. Now."

Someone places an arm around my shoulders. As I look up, I'm face to face with Peter. "I told you I'm going to help you tomorrow," he assures me. "It'll be dark in a couple of hours. Since you're new to the jungle, it wouldn't be a good idea for you to roam around alone at night."

"Peter's right," Toby backs him up. "Stay for the night, eat with us, and tell us everything about you. Any information can help with getting you back on track."

Through the windows higher up in the tree, daylight's already getting dimmer. Maybe it's for the best to camp out with Peter and the Lost Boys and start my exploration early tomorrow morning. I can't do this on my own after all. Hopefully, Mom and Dad will soon be home, so the twins don't panic or something terrible happens to them.

With a nod, I agree and let Peter drag me to the area with the wide table. Loney and Skippy start a fire in the hearth and set up something that looks like a skinned rabbit on a skewer. Obviously we're going to eat roast bunny tonight. I wonder if this is something I'll like.

Chapter 3

The rabbit is excellent, and the best thing about this dinner is there's lots and lots of strawberry milk to wash it all down. Best dinner I ever had.

I help Tami and Toby clear the table, but when I go back for the second load of dishes, Peter grabs my arm and pulls me aside. "What do you say? Shall I give you a quick tour through Neverland before night falls?"

A hike through the jungle? I might spot a possible way to get off this island while exploring. Great! So I don't have to wait until tomorrow after all. "Let me just get my sweater, then we can hike off."

"Hike off..." Peter says, testing the words while I slip into my black sweater.

As I pull it down, an ear-piercing shriek bounces off the walls inside the tree. The little pixie with the pointed ears dashes to her room, leaving a trail of golden dust in her wake. With a loud boom, her door slams shut.

"What in the world—" I don't get to finish my sentence. Each of the boys in the room points at the skull on my sweater. Actually, they look rather ridiculous with their outstretched arms. I make a sheepish face.

"Get Tami out of there and tell her Angel is not a pirate," Peter instructs Sparky, who's running a helpless hand over his buzz cut. "Angel and I have to go now, or it'll get too dark for the tour."

While the boys talk to Tami through the wall, I sidle up to Peter, waiting for him to show me a door that's leading out of this underground tree house. To my total astonishment, he just scoops me up in his arms like earlier this afternoon and rises with me in the air. "What are you doing?" I cry.

He stops and hovers a few feet above the ground. "I thought you wanted to explore?"

"I do. But why do we have to fly again?"

"Because it's the easiest way. Are you scared?"

"Not of flying. I'm just afraid I'll be too heavy for you and you'll drop me." From two hundred feet.

"Yeah, now that you mention it..." Peter sets off toward the opening in the top of the tree, but he's flying like a drunk, wobbling to all sides. "Whoa. Girl, I don't think I can hold you any longer!"

"What?" We're halfway up through the trunk.

"I'm sorry!" He tips from left to right, clearly losing

his balance. "You're just too heavy!"

All of a sudden, his hands are off me, and I plummet. Rowing with my arms is no use. A moment later, gravity flings me into the trampoline and shoots me back up. I gasp as Peter catches me and waggles his brows. He zooms with me out of the tree. The laughter of the Lost Boys follows us.

"Very funny," I growl, wrapping my arms tightly around his neck this time.

Lightheartedly, Peter replies, "Yes, it was." Then he rolls his eyes and grins. "Too heavy for me...? Crazy girl."

The deep orange sun slides low on the horizon as we glide across the sky. The weird thing is, Peter tells me we're starting off north, and if he's to be trusted, the glowing orb is lowering on the east side of the isle.

Frankly, why does this even surprise me?

"Look! Down there's Mermaid Lagoon," Peter says into my ear.

I tilt my head to catch a glimpse. We're right above the north peak of Neverland. The Caribbean-blue sea glistens in the last sunrays of the day. Young women with beautiful long hair and fishtails frolic in the waves, shouting up to us that we should go down and meet them.

"Do you know these girls?" I ask Peter as we descend to the rocky north shore.

"Some of them. Mermaids are usually shy people, but once they get to know you, they sort of warm up." He chuckles, and I'm sure it's about a memory he shares with the mermaids.

Peter sets me down on the shore and waves at the girls in the water. "Hey, Melody! Come and meet my new friend!"

One of the mermaids detaches from the group and pops her head out of the water several feet away from us. She pushes her wet auburn hair behind her ears while the long strands float in the water around her and gives us a shy smile. "Hello, Peter. I haven't seen you in a while. I almost started to believe that Hook had gotten you in the end."

"Never!" Peter laughs and pumps up his chest like a proud rooster. "The day that Hook catches Peter Pan is the day that the sun goes down in the West."

I guess for Neverland this is a working metaphor.

"It would be a sad day for us all," Melody replies. Then her curious gaze wanders to me.

Peter places a hand at the small of my back but his attention is still on the mermaid. "This is my friend, Angel. Dropped from the clouds today." He leans forward a little and adds in a loud whisper, "She got lost."

"Don't they all?" Melody giggles a soul-warming sound and does a back-flip into the water. She comes up a little closer to us next. Near enough to reach for my hand, actually.

"Whoa," is what I say for a greeting. "I'm shaking

hands with a mermaid."

Melody's kelp-green eyes begin to glint with a hint of mischief, and suddenly she tugs hard on my hand. "Come in and play with us!"

I gasp as I lose the ground beneath my feet.

"Oh no!" Peter laughs. "Not today, Mel." He has already wrapped his arm around my middle, preventing me from plunging head first into the waves. "I want to show Angel our treasure as long as we have low tide. Maybe we'll come back tomorrow to play."

Note to self: If you aren't wearing a bathing suit, keep a safe distance from mermaids in the future.

Melody pouts and bats her lashes, but in the next moment she smiles again and splashes water at us with her mighty fishtail before she dives into the waves and swims off. "See you tomorrow!" she shouts over her shoulder.

Yeah. Tomorrow, I think and realize that Peter's still hugging me to his chest. "You do have crazy friends, you know that, Peter Pan?"

"Aw, you'll love them once you grow used to living in Neverland. I promise you'll never want to leave again."

He is right. This dreamy island feels too good to be true. Pixies, houses in trees, and mermaids...who wouldn't want to live in a place like this? On the other hand, back home I have a room of my own and don't have to share a tree with six immature guys and a shrieking pixie. I also miss my sisters, and I'd never trade the adventure of riding on a red double-decker bus for a flight in a lanky guy's arms.

"Are you ready to go?" Peter breaks through my thoughts.

I nod. "Where to?"

Lifting me in his arms again, he pushes off the shore and glides out to the sea. "Treasure island," he informs me. "If you can't fly, you can only reach it with a boat. And then you'll only find it when the tide is out."

"Really? Why?"

"At low tide, the top of the rock protrudes from the water. There's a cave with a hole at the top. We sealed it with a trapdoor. This way no water gets inside when the tide is rolling in. And Hook can't find it, because he can only move out with his ship when the tide is high."

"Very clever," I agree to his smug grin.

We fly about half a mile until we finally reach a rock formation that looks like birthday candles on a cake. Peter lands on the rock closest to us, then he says, "Now second to the right." As if the two of us are weightless, he takes a gazelle-like jump from our rock to the next, and the next. That one's a little bigger than the others. Peter puts me down and starts carrying stones out of the way. I help him and find a square wooden trapdoor beneath. My anticipation rises as he fishes a key from his pocket and unlocks the door. It flaps down on one side. The scent of seawater and rusty copper wafts in my face.

Peter straightens, giving me a teasing look. "Okay, for going down there, you have to actually hug me. The door's too small to carry you through in my arms."

I see what he means, but I feel a little awkward when I sling my arms around his neck and he pulls me closer. Like an embracing couple, we glide down through the porthole. Pitch-black darkness surrounds us. I can't tell how far we really descend, but after a few seconds I feel some sort of ground beneath my feet. Something tingles when I shift my weight from one foot to the other.

"Wait here," Peter orders, then he leaves me alone in the dark. I can hear him scurry around somewhere to my left. Moments later, the warm flames of a torch brighten the cave.

I suck in a sharp breath. "Oh my freaking goodness!"

Peter flies back to me. "You like it?"

In a wild frenzy, I grab his collar, pull him close until our noses touch, and cry, "This is unbelievable!"

Three quarters of the cave floor are covered with heaps and heaps of gold coins, silver goblets, mirrors specked with gemstones, and all kinds of jewelry. I stand on the highest pile, shoving clinking coins in all directions as I drop to my butt and slide down one side. The urge to dive into the heap and swim in the money pool like Uncle Scrooge grips me by the neck, but Peter's voice drags me out of my fascination.

"Come. I want to show you the rest of our treasure."

I make big eyes at him. "There's more?"

"Just a little bit." He pulls me past the hills of gold, toward a huge heavy wooden chest in a corner. When he opens it, thousands of diamonds and multi-colored gemstones glimmer in the torch light.

I run my hands through them, trying to remember to breathe. "Where did you find all this?"

Peter shrugs. "It's Hook's treasure. We stole it from him some time ago."

"You stole a pirate's treasure? Oh my God! Now I understand why this guy is after you."

"Ah." He waves a dismissive hand at me. "If it wasn't for us, Hook would be bored to death by now. He can consider himself lucky we're taking care of him like this."

"Yeah, right." I chuckle and cut an amused glance his way. "You're such a *selfless* person, Peter Pan, aren't you?" He gives me a half-smile back. Then I spot a smaller chest right behind his feet. "What's in there?"

Following the direction of my gaze, Peter lifts the silver chest that is actually no taller than a shoebox from the damp ground and blows across the lid. The dust cloud rising makes me sneeze twice. "Nobody knows what's in there," he tells me. "It's sealed with this iron lock, and Hook still has the key. He carries it on a chain around his neck."

I run my fingers across the dents in the metal. "You've tried to open it?"

"With a stone, with an ax, by tossing it from the top of a mountain, by trying to melt the iron lock…you name it."

The burning marks are still visible and make me laugh. "No chance of getting hold of the key?"

"For years we've been trying to grab that key, but it's the only thing we haven't been able to take off Hook yet."

"I see. Maybe you should bargain with him. Buy the key with part of his own treasure?"

"No way!" Peter flashes a keen grin that makes him look a lot younger. "One day, I'll get hold of that key. You just wait."

I tilt my head but hesitate with my reply. To me it seems like Peter doesn't really want this key so much. It's more the actual adventure of trying to steal it that keeps him motivated. "I hope I'll be here to see it when that day comes," I reply and only then realize how thoughtless that was of me.

"Oh, you can." Peter puts the chest back down and reaches for my hand, tugging me up to the top of the biggest hill of gold. "You can stay here. With the Lost Boys and me. And Tami. Forever."

Forever is not an option for me. "So you can teach me how to hang out in trees and make me a Lost Boy like the others?" I mock Peter and throw a handful of coins at him.

"Why not? You'd be the first Lost *Girl* in Neverland.

And I'd make you a brilliant sword-fighter, too." He tosses some coins back at me, which I dodge. When I straighten again, he gets me in the face with a pearl necklace. "Just think—we could steal Hook's key together."

Remembering how Toby mentioned a cannonball when I first met them this afternoon, I pull a face. "Sounds tempting but...no. I'm not in any way keen on meeting this horrible pirate."

"Aw, you don't know what you're missing out on." Peter bends over and pulls a small silver flute from between the coins. "Neverland is the most wonderful place of anywhere." With the instrument between his fingers, he levitates a few feet up, crosses his legs as though he's sitting on an invisible magic carpet, and starts to play a lovely tune.

I cock my head. "You're a musician?"

"I only know this one melody. Can you play the flute?"

I shrug. So far I haven't tried it, but it can't be too difficult. Peter tosses the flute down to me. Carefully, I place my fingers over the tiny holes in the slim metal pipe and blow, lifting random fingers. The sound is god-awful.

Peter and I grimace at the same time and simultaneously we say, "Nah...!" There's no musical talent whatsoever hidden in me. I toss the flute away and it lands on the treasure heap again with a clink. "Shall we go back?"

Peter nods then grabs me around the waist and flies out through the trapdoor before my cry of surprise even makes it out of my throat. Together we cover the entrance with stones again, then he takes me back to the island. It's already dark when he lands on a hill somewhere close to the jungle. Stretching his limbs, he sprawls out on the ground.

I follow suit and study the many stars in the velvety sky. The grass is still warm from the sun and smells amazing. "I love lying in the grass back home on a warm day like this," I muse into the silent night.

"If you stay, you can do that every day. There's never one day of bad weather in Neverland."

Fascinated, I roll onto my front and gaze at his daring face. "Never?"

"Never, ever! Pixie swear." With his right index finger, he draws a cross over his heart and smirks. "So, what do you think? We have an empty sleeping booth in our tree. It's the perfect size for you." He waggles his brows in this typical teasing manner that I've gotten to know today.

"You're fighting a dirty battle, Peter Pan. And you're absolutely right, Neverland really *is* amazing."

His grin spreads wider at my words.

"But you have a group of fine friends around you," I argue. "You love them all, don't you?" When he nods, I continue, "So you can understand why I must leave? Back in London, my baby sisters are waiting for me. They would miss me terribly if I never came back. And I miss them so much."

For a short moment we are both silent. I wait for Peter to say something, to show me he understands my need to go back. But he says nothing. So I ask, "Why do you want me to stay anyway?"

"Because you're a girl...and girls know how to tell stories."

"Stories? That's it?" Somehow I feel a little disappointed by his answer.

"Well, yeah." He shrugs and laces his fingers behind his head, looking back at the sky. "I think it's cool to have someone to tell you stories before bedtime."

I do know many stories, and the twins love me reading them picture books every night before bedtime. Come to think of it, what was the last story I read to them? Was it Little Red Riding Hood? I'm hooked on that thought, because the harder I try to remember, the more the answer seems to drift away from me. Just like my name.

Next to me, I hear Peter sigh. "None of us boys know any good stories, and Tami...well, she's really not the kind to sit at your bedside and tell a tale." He snorts. "She would just dip us all in pixie dust."

It seems so odd for a guy his age to listen to stories. Maybe it has something to do with his past. His life back in his real home? I go for a random guess. "Did your mother read you stories before bedtime when you were little?"

"I don't remember the time before I came to the jungle," he answers, his tone stark and distant. He sounds so hurt and defensive that my breath freezes in my lungs for a shocked second.

"I'm sorry," I whisper after a while. "I didn't mean to get too personal."

"You weren't. It's just what it is. You don't remember your name; I don't remember where I come from. End of story."

I don't like his sudden change of mood. Mostly because I feel sad for him when he lays out cold facts like this. What's more, I feel like he's not being completely honest with me right now. Maybe a smile and a gentle poke in the ribs can tease out the happy Pan again. "You were right before, Peter," I mock him, wrinkling my nose. "You *are* a lousy storyteller."

Eventually a laugh slips from his lips and he shoves playfully against my shoulder. I shove back, and he shoves again. This time I tip sideways, but I can't let him get away with this, so the shoving continues until we both roll in a bundle down the hill. Our joint laughter echoes around us.

By the time we reach the bottom, I'm dizzy. The world keeps turning around me for a minute. Then I realize I'm straddling Peter's stomach, hands braced on his chest. He grabs my upper arms to steady me. On his right arm, there's a fading scar that I haven't noticed before. It runs from his elbow upward und disappears under the sleeve of his t-shirt. From the looks of it, this must have been a painful wound a long time ago. Because of his earlier mood swing when I asked him about his past, I decide not to question him about it just yet.

Smiling instead, I find his blue, blue eyes that are focused on mine. I can tell he really wants me to stay in Neverland. Not for the sake of getting a good story told. But because he sees something in me that he seems to like. Not my musical talent, that's for sure.

I must have been staring at him for a minute too long, because his brows come together in a frown and he cocks his head. "You okay?"

"Um...sure—" My smile is blown away by something happening in the distance. "Holy crap!" I jump off Peter and stumble up.

Peter is by my side in an instant. He takes on a fighting stance, scanning around me. "What is it?"

"Over there!" I point south, or what I think is south, to the middle of the island. My hand trembles. "A volcano!" And it's erupting.

Peter lets out a long breath. "Ah, you scared the crap out of me. I thought Hook found us."

Turning to him, I feel the blood draining from my

head and my voice takes on an insanely calm edge. "There's a freaking volcano exploding, and you're all relaxed?"

"Would you rather I pee my pants like a girl?" He laughs at me, but then he takes my hand and pulls me down to the ground. "Come, sit. You'll like this."

Like watching a volcano erupt and extinguish half of the isle? I doubt it. Peter doesn't let go of my hand, and though he's slim and appears fragile, he is strong, so I sit with him and train my gaze on nature's furious display of fireworks.

Molten lava slowly creeps over the edge of the opening in the earth. Only the color doesn't seem right. It looks like someone melted gold in there, powdered some pixie dust on it and is now shoveling it out of the high rock. And then, with a bombastic fizzling, a rainbow shoots out of the volcano. In a high arch, it races east over Neverland and dips into the sea, where it gets swallowed by the waves.

"Oh my God, how beautiful..." I mumble.

Peter leans in to me and speaks in my ear. "You think that was nice? Just wait and see."

Quickly, I move my gaze to his face so close to mine then back to the volcano. Already the next glowing rainbow erupts from it. And another. And another. For at least three minutes, the mountain in front of us keeps spitting the most wonderful arches of glimmering colors.

They zoom in all directions, each of them landing in the sea where they brighten the water and finally fade away.

"Cool, huh?" Peter says. I nod. Then he pulls something out of the chest pocket of his shirt. When he holds his hand out to me and opens his fist, there's a little heart-shaped ruby on his palm.

The rainbows completely forgotten, I stroke my fingertips over the gem's smooth surface. "This is lovely," I breathe.

Peter gives me a warm smile. "Take it. It's yours."

"Mine?"

"It's a present."

"Did you take this from your treasure?"

"M-hm." He nods slowly. "Welcome to Neverland, Angel."

A little uncertain, I take the stone from Peter's hand. It's heavier than it looks and surely would make for a beautiful necklace. "Thank you, Peter." I place a chaste kiss on his cheek and behold the beautiful ruby for another endless moment, then I tuck it in my pocket to keep it safe.

Inside the pocket, my fingers brush against something and I go stiff.

"What's up?" Peter asks me.

"Nothing," I murmur. I already know what's in my pocket before I pull out the one-by-two-inch piece of paper.

"Travelcard," Peter reads out loud as he leans over my shoulder to inspect my personal, tiny treasure. He makes a quirky face and adds, "To London."

A wave of fear and homesickness hits me. I'm definitely not on any normal island somewhere in the world. Where I landed is a place that shouldn't exist. What if I can never get away from here again? Never get back home?

Bile clogs my throat. I stand up and walk a few steps away from Peter, clutching the card with both hands.

"Is this a map for you to find London?" Peter's voice is close behind me. "Can you use this to go home?"

I turn around and face him, clearing my throat. "No. I used this yesterday. It's a train ticket. I went to the city to buy a birthday present for my sisters."

"The Lost Boys can become your brothers if you stay. And Tami will be like a sister to you." With narrowed eyes, he looks at me, angling his head. A muscle ticks in his jaw. "You don't have to go back."

I hesitate and reach out for his hand, but he pulls it away. I don't like seeing him depressed. "Please understand, Peter. Neverland is your home, not mine. How would you feel if you landed in the middle of a city you don't know and you couldn't ever see the Lost Boys again?"

A couple of silent seconds tick away. Suddenly Peter straightens and his face takes on a hurt expression. "Fine.

Go back to your *London*. I don't care."

"Peter—"

He flies up a few feet, then hovers for a second and scowls down at me. "Good luck!" An instant later, he zooms away.

"This isn't funny, Peter!" I shout after him and wait a few seconds, but nothing appears out of the dark. Clenching my hands into fists at my sides, my whole body tenses. "Peter Pan! Come back! *Please...!*"

He's already too far away to hear me. I'm left by myself in Neverland. Fantastic.

Chapter 4

I cross my arms and grit my teeth. *Stupid, ignorant boy!* I'll never find my way back to the tree house alone through the jungle. Even if I did, I probably wouldn't be welcome anymore. Since plan A is cancelled, I look around, weighing my options. Plan B is to camp outside. That's not how I intended to spend the night, wandering around on a strange island with no idea of where I am, but this is my best bet.

Behind me is the jungle, in front are rows of hills. It's probably best to find a place beneath a tree where I can overlook the area and still have my back protected from whatever danger creeps through the thicket at night.

"I'm not a coward," I mumble as I sneak closer to a mahogany tree. "Darkness doesn't scare me." My teeth start to chatter. Okay, maybe it does.

The grass rustles under my feet. An owl hoots in the

distance. Sliding down with my back scraping along the rough tree trunk, I try to stay alert and watch for anything that's moving around me. My arms wrapped tightly around my knees, I inhale deeply, filling my lungs with courageous breaths. This is Neverland. The land of treasures and pixies and rainbows. *Nothing to be afraid of.*

But it's also the land of Hook. That name looms in my mind. Captain of the pirates. Ugly as hell, with a silver hook on his arm. Did he lose his hand and somehow replace it with a hook for a weapon? What if he finds me in this thick jungle and slices me with his hook from my belly to my nose?

Jeez, where did that thought come from? I shake it off and concentrate on something nicer: the feeling of golden pixie dust between my fingers and the vision of hundreds of rainbows shooting across Neverland. Yeah, with that picture in my mind I manage to calm down my racing heart. I close my eyes. But with that damn owl still hooting and other nocturnal sounds along with the darkness, it creeps me out.

Jumpy like a rabbit, I sit through the night and pray that the dark clouds shrouding the moon aren't loaded with rain. Peter said there's never one day of bad weather in Neverland. I hope he's right.

My back is stiff and my butt hurts from sitting, so at one point I just tip over to lie on the ground, rest my cheek on my arm and finally sink into a dreamless sleep.

ANNA KATMORE

What feels like minutes later, I wake up again, but the dark has already made room for a bright blue sky. The warm sun shines down at my face. With a good stretch, blood rushes to my numb limbs and my arms and legs no longer feel like dead twigs attached to my body. Yawning louder than a cougar, I get up and dust off the rest of my makeshift bed from my clothes.

My stomach rumbles. I'm hungry as hell, but what's really killing me is my bone-dry throat. I could drink up a lake...if I found one anyway. I didn't see one yesterday, when Peter carried me above Neverland. But the image of the seaport presses into my mind. Maybe I should try to make my way south. There'll certainly be food and water, and who knows, maybe even a ship that sails off this island. Someone surely knows which direction London is.

With my stomach grumbling, I wander off toward the grassy hills separating me from the seaport. As I climb them one by one, beads of sweat form on my forehead. My tongue sticks to the roof of my dry mouth. I'm ready to suck the dew from the grass if necessary, just to get one drop of water. Then, on the fifth hill, the sound of rippling water drifts to me.

A rush of joy quickens my heartbeat. I climb the last few steps and can eventually see the little river rolling though the valley in front of me. My legs develop their own will and carry me down too fast. At the bottom, I stumble and lose balance. Like an avalanche I come down hard and land with a splash in the river.

Not bothering to step out of the shallow water, I sit up and take a few deep breaths to calm myself. Wonderful water! I drink my fill and dip myself under once more to get the dust and jungle filth off me. When I'm done with my sketchy bath, I feel invigorated and ready to walk on. I wade to the other side and climb out.

It's not far anymore. From the top of the last hill, I could already make out the sea and some rooftops. Minutes later, the sounds of the port carry to me and cheer me on to walk faster. It feels like a one-hundred-pound stone is lifted off my chest when the dreamy little port comes into view.

Leaving the hills behind, I walk down a cobblestone street, welcoming the hardness of a street under my feet. Man, it was about time to get out of the wilderness and into civilization. A deeply relieved sigh escapes my lips.

Houses of multiple colors line the street. Some have Venetian balconies and double-wing doors. Others are simpler with flower pots placed next to the doors and beneath windows. The first people I see are a couple of ladies, dressed in bell-bottomed gowns of burgundy and frog-green silk. They carry parasols, but only the woman in red uses hers as shelter from the sun. I want to ask them about a passenger ship, but when I get closer, I see the fear in their faces. Hurriedly, they lift their dresses, exposing their booted ankles, and flit into a narrow alley to my right.

Scratching my head, I pivot. Was it me? Do I stink? No, can't be, I decide after sniffing the sleeves of my sweater, which the sun had dried by now like the rest of my clothes. Then it dawns on me that my sweater must be the reason. Oh darn. Tami was scared as hell when she saw the skull on the front yesterday. These women must think I'm a pirate, too.

To avoid any more misunderstandings, I pull the sweater off over my head and wrap it around my waist, with the image hidden. Tying the sleeves to the front, I walk on and come to what looks like the Main Street filled with people hurrying about. Beyond it spreads the mighty ocean. I speed up and slip into the crowd, where I clearly stand out with my jeans and snug-fitting tee. Although not all are dressed as elegantly as the ladies from two minutes ago, this fashion is clearly from a different time. Maybe from the past century or earlier? One can easily distinguish these people's status by their clothing and style of hair. The rich women wear their hair in updos, decorated with overworked hats, and their gowns cover almost every inch of skin from their neck down to their toes. The poorer folks are wrapped in linen, some even walking barefoot. I feel like I burst in on the set of *Downton Abbey.*

Though everyone still gives me strange sideways glances as they pass me, none of them back away. I fluff up my hair and paste on a friendly smile, then I walk up to a young woman carrying a fruit basket. Her naked feet are smudgy and she might have cooties, but she looks friendly when she hands a pea to a small boy at the side of the street.

"Excuse me, ma'am." I stop right in front of her and tilt my head a little.

"Aye," she says, eyeing me from head to toe.

"Do you know how I can get off this island?"

"With a boat, I'd say." Her gaze glides up to my face and she starts to smile, too, although hers seems skeptical. "But where would you be going, lass? There's nothing but deep, blue sea out there." Holding the basket with one arm, she sweeps the other to the right toward the waves sloshing against the port.

My spirit sinks at her answer, and uncertainty creeps into my voice. "I need to get to London."

"London? Sorry lass, ain't never heard of a place called that." She purses her lips. "Per chance you mean the Indian camp at the east side of the isle?"

Pinching my eyes shut, I release a pained breath. I definitely don't mean an Indian camp. "No, but thanks anyway."

The girl nods, but before she walks off, I grab her arm and ask, "Can I buy an apple?" It must be early afternoon already, I'm starving.

She rubs her palm clean on her simple gray gown,

then holds out a deep red apple to me. "That's half a doubloon."

I have no idea what a doubloon is, but I always carry some change in my pockets. I fish out two one-pound coins and seventy-five pence.

"What is this?" the young woman demands, pulling back the fruit.

"We use this to pay for goods in London."

"Your coins have no value here."

Wringing my hands, I shift my weight uncomfortably from one leg to the other. "I'm sorry, I don't have anything else to give you." Of course, there's a fat ruby sitting in my pocket, but that'd be a ridiculously high price for an apple.

The girl puckers her lips again. Her gaze wanders down to the sweater tied around my waist. "You can have two, if you give me that," she offers.

Ugh. "I don't think you'd be happy with it," I whine.

She shrugs one shoulder and places the apple back into her basket. "My sister needs something new to wear. Take it or leave it. Your choice."

My stomach hurts from hunger. I don't really have much of a choice here. "Fine." Loosening the knot of the sleeves, I sigh and pray that she won't freak out when she sees the pirate image on the front. But all my praying is in vain. As soon as I hold the sweater out to her, she gives a shriek, nearly splitting my eardrums, and dashes away in the opposite direction, taking her food basket with her.

Luckily for me, the shiny red apple falls out from her basket and rolls down the street. I don't pay attention to her or anyone else at this moment but race after the fruit. If I can't catch it within the next few seconds, it'll drop into the waves. And then I'm screwed.

People complain and skip out of my way as I chase the rolling red ball. Bending over, I almost reach it. But still, I'm too slow. Someone beats me there.

A black boot stops my apple and traps it under the toe, squishing all my hope in a heartbeat. Moaning, I drop to my knees right in front of that boot. My disappointed expression reflects in the furbished silver buckle.

A hand moves into my vision and claims my meal. I look up into the face of a young man. When he straightens again, I straighten with him. With a couple of feet between us, he gives me an unsettling once-over, surely because of my unusual clothes. According to his dark purple brocade coat and clean black leather pants, and no less because of the demeaning look he gives me, I rate him upper-class.

Sharp blue eyes stare at me from under his over-long, bright blond hair that looks as if the wind had ruffled it. His jaw and upper lip sport a dusting of stubble in the same sun-kissed shade. His brows come together in a frown. Maybe because he's used to lower-class people backing away from him. Well, I don't.

"That is *my* apple," I state with the steadiest voice I can manage when his glare actually causes the little hairs at the back of my neck to stand on end. I hold out my hand, palm up.

The young man purses his lips as though he doesn't believe his ears. Then one side of his mouth slowly tilts up as he slides the apple into the wide pocket of his coat. He looks straight into my eyes for another intense second, then he starts laughing, turns on the heels of his well-worn boots and walks away.

"Damn wretch," I mumble and trudge off—not after him but over to a low stone wall surrounding what looks like an abandoned fishing hut with boards nailed across the windows and door. Exhaustion eats at me and my stomach feels like it's munching on itself in hunger.

One foot placed on the crumbling wall, the other dangling, I sit and lean against a jamb stone behind me. My hair snags on the rough surface as I tilt my head up and I wince. A clear blue sky is the only thing in my vision for a while. If this is all but a dream, I'd do anything to wake myself up. Maybe I should find Melody again and ask her to pull me underwater until I run out of air. One can't die in a dream, right? It would wake me up for sure. Only there's the rub: if this isn't a dream, I'd be screwed.

I sigh and wish I could hug my little sisters. What if I never see them again? Or Mom and Dad and Miss Lynda?

Pissing off Peter wasn't my best bet. He might have eventually helped me figure out what to do. Maybe he'll stop sulking at some point and come find me. He can't really be mad because I don't want to spend the rest of eternity in Neverland.

Realizing there's something cold in my hand, I look down and find the ruby heart in my palm. I stroke it a few times, then turn it over and over and finally hold it against the sky. The warm sunrays break in the many facets and cast a swarm of red dots on my t-shirt. They dance when I tilt the gem back and forth.

My gaze starts to wander out to the waves lashing against the concrete port then back to land and over the finely dressed people busying themselves on this romantic marketplace of a different age. Some buy food or bales of silk, others drink the day away in front of pubs. The throaty laughter of a few men draws my attention. They are seated on small stools around a barrel that serves them as some sort of poker table. I stiffen. In their midst sits the apple-stealing scamp.

He's not laughing with the others. In fact, I wonder if he even heard what they're laughing about because, with his elbows propped on the top of the barrel and his fingers steepled under his chin, he seems deeply in thought. And unless he's interested in the run-down hut behind me, his focus is on me.

I hold his stare for just a moment, my teeth clenched,

ANNA KATMORE

then I deliberately look away. This guy can go sit on train tracks. He sure has more money than is good for him and still he couldn't spare me one darn apple.

Continuing to roll the ruby between my fingers, I try to come up with a plan for my departure off this island. Obviously, airplanes aren't an option, but maybe one of the few ships harboring farther down this promenade will get me back. Although they don't seem like they've been out on the sea in a long time. People walk on and off the decks of those ships, but it looks more like they've been converted into shops or pubs rather than transportation.

"You hold a diamond worth more than half of the town, and you're running after an apple. What's the deal?"

I tilt my head to the soft male voice. Leaning against the streetlamp a few feet away, the thief in his purple brocade coat gazes at me with an intrigued half-smile. His arms are folded across his broad chest and one of his feet rests on the iron post behind him.

My first reaction is to quickly shove the stone into my jeans pocket and hide it from his view. "I don't see how that is any of your business," I snap.

He reaches into his pocket and without warning tosses the apple at me. "Make it my business."

I catch the fruit with both hands and sort of panic, immediately biting into it before he can reclaim it. Oh dear mother of God, this tastes delicious. The saliva in my mouth mingles with the apple's juice and I swallow, quickly taking another bite.

"You're a visitor."

"What gave me away?" I ask around the piece in my mouth and give him a cynical look.

He comes over and sits down in front of me. He doesn't bother to dust off the wall with a tissue first, like I expected from someone of his status. So maybe he's not a haughty little prince after all. Instead of answering my question he counters, "Where do you come from?"

Now that he's abandoned that demeaning scowl from earlier, he looks a lot less intimidating. And since he seems interested in my story, maybe he'll help me. Licking the juice off my lip, I study him for another moment, but when he lifts his brows, prompting me to continue, I tell him, "I come from a different island."

"Really? What's it called?"

"Gr...ah..." I snap my fingers twice and roll my eyes skyward, struggling to get the name out that's on the tip of my tongue. *Agh.* Why can't I remember it all of a sudden? I know I told it to Peter last night. But it's just like with my own name. The information seems completely eradicated from my memory.

Feeling awkward to the bone, I move my gaze back to the man in front of me and say with a firm voice, "The name of the island doesn't matter. I live in London, a huge city there."

"Oh. Okay." He shrugs. "I've never heard of it."

"Yeah, I thought so. No one here seems to have. Which doesn't make it any easier for me to go back there."

"You want to go back?"

"Of course!"

"Then why did you come to Neverland in the first place?" His face is still all innocence and intrigue. He swings one leg over the wall so he sits astride it and braces his hands on the space between us. "Isn't it irrational to go to a place where there's no way to leave again if you don't intend to stay?"

"Hey, it wasn't my intention to come here. It was an accident."

He flexes his shoulders. "Ah. I see. Makes all the difference." He sounds like he doesn't believe one word. "And now you're trying to countermand that mistake."

"Accident."

"Right."

"Yes. Sort of. If only I knew whether all this is really *real*," I whine and finish off the juicy apple then throw the apple core in a high arc into the water. "You know, like whether I'm just dreaming or hallucinating."

The man fidgets again in his coat then opens the buttons and frowns, pulling uncomfortably on the collar. "To me it seems real enough. Or I wouldn't feel so compressed in this bloody thing."

Somehow I get the feeling the dress coat isn't what he usually wears. Did he only put it on to impress somebody today? Certainly not the booze buddies at the barrel over there. One of them just tipped over and is now snoring on the hard cobblestone street.

"Can you tell me how to get off this island?" I ask him, not intending to waste any more time on chitchatting. I really have to return to my sisters.

He shrugs. "Ship."

"Do they go out anytime soon?"

Looking over his shoulder, he rubs his neck and drawls, "I don't think so. But I know of a ship outside town. It should be leaving in an hour. If you hurry up, you can make it."

I jump to my feet like an excited puppy. "Which way?"

The young man laughs. A soft sound I wouldn't have expected from him either. "I'll show you, and you can tell me all about this *London* while we walk."

Whatever. I'd even give him a piggyback ride if it meant I'd get back home. At my prompting smile he pushes to his feet then reaches down to the other side of the wall and picks up my fallen sweater, which I forgot in my euphoria.

"*Uh*—no!" I shout. But it's too late. He already shakes it out and of course sees the image of the Caribbean pirate on it. Pursing his lips, he freezes and his eyes go dark. "Really, this is nothing. Just a meaningless image. I swear I'm not a pirate!"

His gaze wanders up over the black fabric and meets mine. Amusement replaces the darkness in his look. One corner of his mouth twitches. "I didn't think you were."

A relieved sigh escapes me.

Stepping out of his rigid composure, he smiles at me, places one hand in the small of my back and steers me to the right. When he hands me the sweater, I tie it—image toward my butt—around my waist again.

We leave the town behind us and the cobblestone street gives way to a narrow dirt road. Occasionally, the waves lap against the rocky shore to my left and a faint spray of water catches my arm. The chill feels welcome against the afternoon heat.

There's nothing in front of us but grassland to one side and the sea to the other. No other port, no ships, not even a boat. I hope we're going to reach this ship before it takes off, and with it—my only chance to go home.

"So, what's your name, lass?" he asks me after some time with an odd notch of amusement in his voice, clasping his hands behind his back as we walk.

"Angel...I think."

"You think?"

I grimace. "It's complicated."

From the corner of my eye I see him turn his head my way, so I look at him too and find him smiling. "I'm sure I can cope," he says.

As we walk so close to each other, I catch a whiff of

seawater and leather on him and wonder if he lives close to the ocean. The note of tangerine underneath strokes my senses. He actually smells nice.

"I don't really know where to start," I say and scratch my head. "See...I live in the real world—" The young man interrupts me by arching one brow. "You know," I explain, "where there are big cities...and traffic...and airplanes. And McDonald's." His second brow follows suit. Right, I'm on the entirely wrong track here. "Let's just say it's a world pretty different from yours, obviously far, far away, if no one here knows of it. I went out on my balcony last night; it was freezing cold. I slipped and fell. Only I never really hit the ground. Instead I was suddenly sky diving to Neverland."

He silently listens. Maybe he has heard of similar cases before.

"Anyway, when I landed here, I remembered everything of my life, just some minor information seems to have gotten lost."

Now he laughs. "Your name is minor information?"

"I...er..." I clasp my hands, then I decide to show him my wrist with the tattoo on it. "I think this is my name, though I have no idea how or when I got this tattoo, or if it's real for that matter."

"It's not," he states in a matter-of-fact tone, surprising me. How can he tell the difference from only one quick look at it? Because I'm stunned silent for a second he adds, "I know a little about tattoos myself. See—" He grabs my wrist and tilts it. His hand is surprisingly callused. "The surface glistens in the sun. No real tattoo does that. The ink should be *in* your skin, not on it. Somebody painted this on you."

Painted it on me? Who would— A sudden smile slips to my face. *Paulina*. She loves these things and is just the girl to make me stick them on my arms. Maybe she did it last night and I just can't remember? What had we been doing all evening anyway?

"Where have you gone?"

Startled out of my musing, I blink and focus on the guy's curious blue eyes.

"It seemed like I'd lost you for a moment. Everything okay?"

"Yeah. I was just trying to remember what really happened right before my accident. My memory feels awkwardly...*spongy*."

Pursing his lips, he lets go of my wrist and clasps his hands behind his back again. "Rumor has it every now and then a stranger comes to Neverland. But they usually don't remember where they come from. They just show up and stay forever."

The corners of my mouth point down. "I've heard about that."

"So you really *do* want to go back."

He sounds like only now does he really believe my

intention. If he didn't before, why show me to a ship that's sailing away from the island? And where is this ship anyway?

A sudden rush of panic swamps me and makes me freeze on the spot. He halts too, a puzzled expression creeping to his eyes. "What's wrong?" he asks, seeming genuinely concerned.

"Do you know who owns this ship that you're taking me to?"

"What do you mean?"

"It's not this *Captain Hook's* ship, is it?"

He pauses for a moment, studying me with his head tilted. A frown knits his brows together as he slowly asks, "Whoever is Captain Hook?"

Phew, I'm safe. If it was Hook's ship, this man would surely know. My shoulders and back relax and I continue walking with him. "I've never met him, but apparently, Hook is a pirate. He's alleged to be the ugliest, meanest and scariest man in Neverland."

"Oh my, if that's the truth, I hope I never cross paths with him."

I smile. "Me, too."

"Well, you don't have to be afraid. I know everyone on that ship. Trust me, you'll be absolutely safe."

I try to calm down and forget about Hook. He's probably just a phantasm after all. I wouldn't be surprised if Peter and his friends made him up just because they were bored or to scare people like me. Now I can actually laugh about Loney's silly suggestion that I was hit by a cannonball when I fell out of the sky. Too funny.

Returning my attention to the man at my side, I ask, "What's your name anyway?"

One corner of his mouth impishly tilts up. Probably because it took me so long to come up with this basic question. Only now I realize I was talking about myself all the time. He waits another second before he answers, "My name's Jamie."

I like how his half-smile grows into a full one. When he doesn't pull this *sharp-eyes, I'm-upper-class* shit, he really is a handsome man. Hard to say how old he is, because the suntan he's sporting makes him look mid-twenties at first sight, but when one looks a little closer, he still bears those boyish lines of someone much younger. Twenty-one or even twenty-two if you stretch it.

His smile eases and is replaced by a curious look. Realizing I stared at his face a fraction too long, I feel an embarrassing heat sneaking to my cheeks. He saves me from this awkward moment when he informs me, "We're almost there," and nods into the distance, where the tip of a mast swaying behind a low hill gives away the location of our destination.

Relief pushes through me. He wasn't lying, there actually *is* a ship. But as we draw nearer, another worry swamps me. "Wait. I have no doubloons on me. Do you think they'll let me on board?"

"I think they will. And if not, you still have a ruby the size of a marble in your pocket. If nothing else, that one should get you anywhere." A hint of ravenousness flashes in his eyes, but it's gone before I can be sure. I was probably mistaken. If he really wanted to steal the ruby from me, he had plenty of time on the way down here.

"Yeah, it should cover the cost of any voyage," I agree. "Although I would hate to give it away. It was a gift from a friend."

"A friend here in Neverland?"

"Yes. His name is Peter."

Jamie suddenly struggles to keep his expression under control. Startled doesn't even begin to describe how he looks. A muscle ticks in his jaw. "Peter...*Pan*?"

"Yes. Do you know him?"

A sluggish smile creeps to his lips. "You could say we're close like...*brothers.*"

"Without Peter I'd be mash in the jungle now," I tell Jamie. "He was the one who saved me from the fall yesterday."

"I'm not surprised. The lost ones usually find him first. There's something about him that pulls you kids in."

The fact he calls me a kid grates on my ego. Partly because of what I learned about Peter and the guys last night. Staying a child forever...*ick*. I'm almost eighteen, I run with the grown-ups now. Babysitting my little sisters every weekend should be proof enough. But I don't let my anger show. Then I stop worrying about it altogether as we reach the top of the hill and I see it.

My ticket home!

My heart steps up a beat at the sight of the ship calmly bobbing on the waves close to the shore. It's taller than I expected, made entirely of cappuccino-brown wood. Its beauty takes my breath away. I can just imagine how Christopher Columbus sailed around the world in a ship like this. Only one of three sails is hoisted—the middle one and obviously the biggest of them all. It's plain white and bloats in the soft breeze.

The front and back part of the ship are higher than the middle, housing exclusive cabins from what I can see. There are small square windows built into them, and some even have drawn curtains. On top of the back quarters must be the bridge. The vacated wheel with the many handles catches my eye even from a hundred and fifty feet away.

A handful of people start bustling around as a guy with a spyglass next to the railing sees us and shouts an unintelligible warning to the others. Could be he told them to wait with the departure, because more passengers are coming on board.

Excited, I walk faster, my eyes almost popping out with wonder. Jamie, who matches my stride, chuckles next to me. When we reach the plateau closest to the ship, I hesitate and crane my neck to stare up, taking in all of it. He pokes me gently in the ribs with his elbow. "It's a mighty fine ship, eh?"

"Stunning," I breathe.

"Then what are you waiting for? Come on." With one hand placed on my back, he leads me around to the long narrow gangplank and has me step on it first. Watching my feet, I warily make my way toward the main deck. The farther I walk, the more the wooden board wobbles under my weight. I can hear Jamie's footsteps right behind me, which gives me a little comfort.

With a quick glance, I assure myself that we're already closer to the ship than to land. But at the same time I catch a glimpse of a very dirty sailor on deck. He wears a torn shirt and a black bandana. A real saber is attached to his belt and a black patch covers his left eye. I stop dead.

Jamie bounces into my back at my sudden halt. His hands come to my waist and keep me steady. "What's up?" he asks into my ear.

I turn my head just slightly, not letting the man out of my sight, and whisper, "Are you sure this is the ship you talked about?"

"Of course."

"Did you see what they're wearing? I think these men are pirates."

"Don't worry," he replies with a chilled laugh. I *do*

worry, though. Goosebumps rise on my skin. I want to get off this gangplank and back on land, but Jamie pushes me forward.

A few more steps and I stand on the wide deck, earning the greedy looks of more men dressed in shabby clothes. One of them flashes a gold-toothed smile at me.

"Jamie?" I croak, my knees turning to rubber. "I think we are on the wrong ship."

"Relax, *Angel*." He makes my name sound like a mocking endearment. The tip of his finger glides down the back of my neck in an uncomfortable caress. "We're exactly where we're supposed to be."

Sucking in a sharp breath, I spin around. Jamie pulls off his brocade coat with now obvious disgust for the cloak and tosses it over the railing. "Ah. Much better!" He flexes his shoulders and releases a deep sigh.

He's only wearing a plain off-white linen shirt now with long sleeves and a laced collar. Jeez, how could I have missed before that this was totally out of character with the fine purple coat? "You—you're one of them," I hoarsely state the obvious. "You're a pirate."

Amusement glistens in his eyes. He gives me a taunting half-smile that freezes the breath in my lungs. "And the ugliest, meanest and scariest of them, too, I was told."

The man with the gold tooth steps up to Jamie and hands him a wide black hat with a single black feather, then he cups his hands around his mouth and shouts, "Get up, ye mangy dogs! The cap'n is on deck!"

"Hook," I breathe.

Jamie rakes a hand through his hair and puts the hat on his head, gazing at me with a wicked gleam in his eyes. His smile turns into a dangerous promise. "Welcome aboard the Jolly Roger."

Chapter 5

I try to rush past him and get off the ship, but Hook captures me easily with one arm around my waist and pulls me back. I fall against his rock-hard chest, away from the gangplank that two of his men pull in.

"Put her out, Smee!" he shouts over my head to another young man dressed completely in black, who appears on the sterncastle. His ginger hair looks shaggy and he wears a red bandana around his neck. First, I think Hook is talking about me and wonder what he means. But moments later the pirate on the bridge yells orders to draw anchor and hoist sails. The ship starts to glide away from the shore.

I'm trapped on the Jolly Roger.

"Let go, you freaking bastard!" Thrashing about, I scream like a snake has wound around my waist instead of his arm. On second thought, Hook is just as bad as a snake.

His mocking laughter rumbles in my ear. "There, there. Who taught you such nasty words, little Miss London?"

My elbow connects with his diaphragm and smacks the damn grin right off his face. I'm free and stumble away. With one hand pressed to his chest, Hook bends forward and pushes out a cough. He clearly underestimated me. This is my only chance, but we're already too far out, and several members of his smudgy crew are blocking my sight to the shore, backing him up. There's no time to think. Frantically, I spin around, dash across the ship and climb onto the railing. Gathering all the power I have inside me, I leap out and plummet fifteen feet into the waves.

The cold water takes me under in a wild spin, determined to smash me against the belly of the ship. Seconds pass, I battle to gain back control of my limbs and orientation. With lungs compressed to the size of tennis balls, I push up from the watery depths and finally break through the surface, sputtering water from mouth and nose, and suck in a lifesaving breath.

"Look what we've got down there, Cap'n!" I hear Smee's faint laughter from deck and turn to find most of the men standing behind the railing, gaping down at me with dirty grins. "A mermaid."

The crowd parts and Hook steps through. Slowly, he

ANNA KATMORE

braces his hands on the railing, leans forward and arches his brow. "Was that really necessary?"

Yeah, it would all be so easy for him if I just played the nice captive. But I don't think so. To get back on land, I have to swim around the ship, so I start paddling and struggle through the water with arms weak from hunger.

"What now? Are you trying to swim away? Back to London?"

I don't answer Hook's amused shout but swim faster. The tied sleeves around my waist loosen and my sweater slips away. Hastily I reach underwater to grab it, but I can't get a hold. If the situation wasn't so dire, the fact the sea swallowed my *Pirates of the Caribbean* sweater would have made me laugh. I swim on.

"Come on, Angel. You'll never make it. If we don't catch you, the sharks will."

Refusing to let his taunting words put me in a panic, I grit my teeth and ignore him.

"Aaaaangeeeel…!" He keeps pace with me, walking slowly along the railing and has fun at it, too. He sounds like he's talking to an infant when he tells me, "We're seventeen men and a ship against you. Why can't you just be nice and surrender? Be my guest!"

Guest, hah! He must be bonkers. But he soon seems to reach the limits of his patience and growls, "Smee! Fish her out!"

No matter how fast I pedal, I can't escape the fishing

net that's being cast over me then. As they pull the strings of the net together, I'm tossed about and they haul me back on board like the catch of the day. My struggling is in vain. I land like a flopping catfish on deck.

Two men with their shoulder-length hair tied in a braid grab me by my arms and yank me to my feet. "What we do with her, Cap'n?" the one to my left asks Hook. He wears an earring the size of a bracelet and both his forearms display mermaid tattoos. With his wrinkled skin and the gray streaks in his black hair, he looks to be the oldest man on board, though I doubt he's older than his early forties. He smells like rotten fish.

"Tie her to the mast, Fin." Hook's order is cold, emotionless. Arms folded over his chest, he waits until I stand pressed with my back against the tallest mast on the ship, my arms yanked to the back of the pole and tied with a rough rope chafing my skin. All the time, we never break eye contact. When the pirate called Fin is done and my hands are secured, Hook waves him away.

A cold aura surrounds the captain when he moves his hands down to his belt and slowly walks over to me. The letter J is engraved in the silver buckle. Only on a second look do I realize it's not a letter but a hook. And suddenly I wonder why he still has both his hands. The Lost Boys said he had a hook on his right arm. Apparently, he doesn't.

"Why are you holding me prisoner on your ship?" I

snap when he's only a couple of steps away.

"Because you're of great value. And because you have something that belongs to me."

"Yeah? And what would that be?"

The captain takes another step forward, closing the distance between us until we share the same breath. "My heart," he says in a strangely soft way and caresses my cheek with his fingertips.

What the heck— Too baffled, I don't get out a single word.

His eyes stay warm when his mouth twitches into a greedy grin. He lowers his hands to my hips then strokes them gently down to my thighs. "Ah, here it is." His grin grows wider and this time his eyes match it with a dark glint. Violating my intimate zone without warning, he shoves his hand into the right pocket of my wet jeans. I gasp. But he withdraws it a moment later—and with it, the ruby from Peter Pan.

"Give that back!" I strain to get my wrists freed. "It was a gift! You goddamn thief!"

Hook tilts the gemstone in the sun, studying it with a frown that he directs at me next, and drawls, " How...little Angel...can I be the thief when *you* carry something that's rightfully mine?"

I hesitate with my answer and lower the level of my voice. "I didn't steal it. Peter gave it to me."

"Yes. Peter Pan," he says through gritted teeth. "The

one damn bug that has been annoying me for decades."

Did he say decades? Oh my God, how long has Peter really been a teenager? And the entire island never aged a day? But then I realize I'm in deeper trouble than just stuck in a timeless area. I'm stuck on a ship that's run by a ruthless captain and his ugly-as-hell pirates. I need a plan.

"Fine. You have back what you wanted. Now take off these ropes and let me go."

A spine-chilling chuckle sounds from his throat. "Oh, Angel, Angel. You really don't understand, do you? This little ruby is only a pebble of my original treasure. Heaps and heaps of gold, silver and diamonds." He holds the gem between two fingers in front of my eyes, tilting his head, and studies me closely. Then he straightens and quickly wraps his fist around the stone. He tucks it into his pocket. His voice loses all warmth. "But I'm sure you already know this. You've seen it, haven't you?"

Not daring to even blink, I shake my head.

"Where. Is. My treasure, Angel?"

"I don't know what you're talking about," I shout, just short of a new panic. Peter Pan trusted me when he showed me the cave. I can't betray him. Not even after he abandoned me last night. "Peter gave this to me yesterday. We sat on a hill, watched the freaking rainbow volcano, and he pulled the ruby from his shirt pocket. There sure weren't heaps and heaps of gold hidden in *there*!"

He frowns, as if deliberating whether I was actually

telling the truth. Spewing out a curse, he finally leaves me alone and walks to Smee who, until now, watched us silently from the railing. "What do you think, Jack? Is she lying?" Hook asks him in a lowered voice.

"I don't know." Smee casts a brief glance my way and scratches his left brow that's parted by an old, whitening scar. I can't stop wondering how many battles he's already fought in the body of a twenty-year-old over the years. "A reckless jump off a ship?" he continues. "She seems like a tough one. Mighty fine blow she aimed at you before. I wouldn't put it past her to lie to save the brats."

"What do you suggest? Torture?"

I suck in a sharp breath at the thought of being hurt by these men, but both ignore me. Jack Smee raises an eyebrow at his captain. "She's a kid, that one."

Grimacing, Hook rubs his lower chest. "According to the blow that so obviously impressed you, she's not."

"Still. She's a *girl.*"

His lips pursed, Hook gives me a thoughtful look. "She's of no use to us, if she doesn't reveal where the treasure is." With resoluteness in his move, he turns back to Smee. "May as well let her walk the plank."

"What?" We've sailed away from the island at a good speed for the past half hour. There's nothing but water around us. "I don't even know where the island is! You can't expect me to swim back to the shore!"

Hook closes his eyes for a second longer and the

corner of his mouth twitches up in a peculiar way. "Oh, I don't." He draws nearer, the heels of his boots clacking eerily on the wooden deck. "We let you get off here and the sharks will do the rest."

Over his shoulder, I catch a glimpse of multiple dark triangular fins cutting through the water. They hadn't been there a few minutes ago. We must be out really far. I start to tremble. Is this the right time to tell him I do know where Pan's treasure is? Peter would hate me, and I mean *really* hate me, not just be miffed because I'm not aiming to stay in Neverland. And once I tell Hook, what guarantee is there he doesn't push me off the plank anyway? Once he has the treasure, I'm definitely *of no use* to him.

Freaking hell, what am I supposed to do?

Jack Smee loosens the rope around my wrists and pushes me a few steps away from the mast, then he ties my hands in the small of my back once more. As he leads me through the two rows of men, the crew cheers in anticipation of me being a shark meal.

Three men set up a board on the railing that leads out into the sea. Smee pulls me to a stop right in front of it and turns me to face Hook who's standing with his hands clasped at his back and flashes a delighted grin.

"Any last words?" he asks me.

"Go to hell, you freaking...filthy...godforsaken..."

With a single step, he closes the distance between us.

Our noses almost touch as he dips his head and brushes a strand of my hair behind my ear. "Darling, the word you're looking for is pirate." And there it is again, the dangerous gleam in his eyes. Ruthlessly, he grabs my upper arm and pushes me onto the plank.

One of the men fetches a broom and pokes me forward with it until I stand on the very edge. My knees wobble, my heart races like a machine gun. Only a few hours ago, I considered finding Melody and making her drown me in the sea to wake up. Now, with the sharks only a few meters beneath me, this plan doesn't seem so brilliant after all. But in the end it might be the solution to all my problems. I'm stuck in some strange dreamland, and dying would get me out. Wake me up. Bring me back. I close my eyes...

"Wait!"

Hook's sudden yell startles me. I look over my shoulder.

"Take her back in, Smee. I have an idea." That's all he says before he strides toward the ship's stern and disappears in a cabin beneath the bridge.

I let go of a long sigh of relief as Smee takes me back on board. He leaves me in the care of the man who smells like rotten fish then follows his captain.

James Hook

Oh, Peter Pan, this time I'm going to squish you beneath my boot.

Slamming the door behind me in irritation, I stride to the wide wooden desk in front of the row of tall windows overlooking the sea. In this study I usually plan battle strategies with Smee, but now I pull the ruby heart from my pocket, drop it on the desk together with my hat and pace the room.

You dare give away part of my treasure? I'll teach you a lesson you won't forget, you nasty little piece of work.

Removing the cufflinks from my shirt, I yank it over my head and toss it on the swivel chair between the desk and the windows. In front of the tall mirror in the corner I stop and brush my fingers over my chest. There's a bruise forming on the right side. Damn, that girl has some strength in her. And an unbreakable will, too. The whereabouts of my treasure is still unknown. Not even in the eye of death did she succumb but instead shot down my excellent plan. None of the scared rats outside would have shown such courage. Well, probably Smee, but he's the only one.

I close my fist around the golden key dangling from a chain around my neck and make a promise. I will find my treasure—together with the little chest. And then I'll stop this whole remaining a child shit.

A rap sounds on the door.

"Come in, Jack!" I say, knowing it's my first mate, because he's the only one who I allow in here.

Smee steps in and shuts the door behind him, but not fast enough. Over his shoulder, I catch a glimpse of Angel in the middle of my crew. The men are teasing her, but none of them lay a hand on the girl. And they won't. Not if they know what's good for them.

"James?" Jack pulls me out of my staring at the now-closed door. "You look concerned. Is everything all right?"

"I find it highly disturbing to have a lass on my ship," I admit through a clenched jaw. This is pirates' domain, for God's sake. You don't toss a kitten into a cage of ravenous wolves.

"Then why did you bring her on board?"

"She had my ruby. There was no other choice. And when she said she got it from Pan, I was ready to bet my right leg on him coming to save her from the sharks."

Smee leans against the door and folds his arms over

his chest. "Yeah, I thought so, too. What do you think, why didn't he come?"

I shrug and pull on the black shirt I left on the ottoman this morning in exchange for the finer one to go to town with. "She was alone when I met her. Maybe Peter thought she had already gone back home. The ruby could have been a gift of farewell."

"I knew you wouldn't toss her to the sharks in the first place, but what's the idea you spoke of? You have another plan?"

"Maybe she can't lead us to the treasure." I let a smug smile enter my face. "But she sure knows where Peter Pan and his friends are hiding."

"You want her to lead us through the jungle? Excellent idea. If she stayed with them for some time, she certainly knows where all the traps are and can lead us around."

I nod. "Give them orders to return to the isle and have four men get ready to go ashore with us at nightfall. The rest will stay aboard to defend the ship."

Smee leaves immediately. I lock the ruby in a drawer of my desk and put my hat back on, pulling the brim lower down my forehead.

Your last hour has come, Peter Pan.

Chapter 6

We have been walking along a path leading away from the shore for at least an hour and a half with night surrounding us, and still no one wants to tell me where we're heading. Smee and Hook flank me, four pirates following us. They hollered and made dirty jokes for the better part of this journey, but since we reached the jungle a few minutes ago, their chatting has gradually ceased. Now they are so silent I peek over my shoulder to make sure they're still there. And only in the dim moonlight can I make out their shapes.

Hook didn't say a word the entire time. He seemed deep in thought. Smee, apparently too scared to disturb his captain in his musing, was silent too. Or maybe they just didn't want to discuss whatever they planned to do in front of me? However, while Hook set a fast pace at the beginning—I could hardly match his steps without jogging alongside him—I realize that his entire body has become cautious since we entered the thicker jungle, as if expecting trouble.

"Light a torch," he orders Smee.

His companion pulls a long piece of wood from the bag he brought and kindles a flame with a match that he strikes on the sole of his boot. The burning torch casts a circle of comforting light around us. "Which way?" Smee asks then.

"I don't know." Hook shrugs. "Why don't we ask our little Angel?" His gaze skates to me. "If you'd be so kind and lead the way, Miss London."

My mouth sags open and I surely make wider eyes than a koala bear at him. "You want me to lead you through the jungle?"

"And show us to Pan's hideout, yes. You're the only one who knows where all the traps are."

I squeeze my eyes closed and would have pinched the spot between them, but I can't because my wrists are still tied at my back. "What traps?" I say through gritted teeth.

"The ones Peter Pan and the Lost Boys set up for us, of course," Jack Smee explains with a parody of a smile.

Last night haunts me. If there really are traps in the jungle, I was lucky I didn't venture inside alone. "I don't know of any traps! And I don't know how to get to his place either! We never hiked through the jungle." Biting pain shoots up my arms as I struggle against the rope around my wrist. It's no use; they're awfully tight. "If you know him so well, it's probably not a secret to you that he's capable of flying. And he does it a lot!" My head starts to ache. I feel groggy and tired. Stepping aside, I lean against a tree. "Go find the way yourself."

"You gave us a convincing show on the plank," says Hook. "This time we won't let you get away so easily. If you don't know where the traps are, then you better start praying, because you *will* lead us through the jungle and to Pan's den."

I want nothing more than to lie down and rest. When is this nightmare going to end? My legs feel like rubber and I can barely see straight. What wouldn't I give for Peter to find me and lift me in his arms again, flying me back to their tree. The cozy sleeping booths inside are all I can think of right now.

An idea pops up in my mind. Everything is quiet out here. My yell should carry over miles. I suck in a deep breath then scream, "Peeeeteeer!" with all the strength I have in my lungs. "Peter Pa—"

Hook grabs my arm, spinning me around. My back is flush against his front and his big hand presses over my mouth. "If you want to survive the night, you better stop this shit," he growls in my ear.

Only when my thrashing and whimpering cease does he let go, turning me so he can glare at me. "Good. Now go and lead the way around the traps. And Angel...I swear if you're trying to trick us, you're going to regret it."

"How can I trick you? I don't know the way nor where the traps are!" Tears spring to my eyes but I blink them back. "I'll be the first to fall into one. And you won't even take off the bonds."

"Better *you* fall into one than *us*," he says coldly. But then he spins me around and surprises me as he cuts the ties with a knife he pulled from inside his boot. "Now go ahead and lead the way."

I rub the burn from my wrists, staring stunned into his detached eyes. He must know I'm telling the truth...and he still wants me to go first. "You're a ruthless man, Jamie," I whisper through a constricted throat.

If I thought his expression was cold before, I wasn't prepared for how he looks at me now. So full of loathing it ignites a shudder of fear down my spine. He takes the two steps to me, blocking out my view of Smee and the others. His hard gaze freezes the breath in my lungs. "If you ever call me that again in front of my crew, this"—he holds up the rope and slices through it with the knife—"will be your throat."

I gulp.

Tilting his head, he demands in a dangerously soft voice, "Do I make myself clear?"

"Yes, Captain," I croak.

"Fine. And now go."

My entire body shuddering a number seven on the

Richter scale, I turn away from him and take one wary step after the other deeper into the jungle. For the first time in my life I'm really scared. Scared of what lies in front, and even more so of the man behind me. I don't want to be in Neverland anymore. I want to be back home. I want to hug Brittney Renae and tickle Paulina until I hear her lovely laughter again.

The sound of their voices echoes in my mind from far, far away. I hear them call my name. Call me back. I want to go. I so badly want to close my eyes and just go home.

I don't know if it's sheer dumb luck or if there really aren't any traps, but I manage to hike on for another hour without getting caught in anything. We cross a small clearing, and I look up to the sky, wishing upon a star that this nightmare is over soon.

And then there's a rustling to my right.

As the light from the torch behind me goes out, I spin around and stare into the dark. All the pirates are gone and I am alone. I know they must be somewhere nearby, hiding in the underbrush. *Why?*

"Angel?"

I turn to a voice I didn't dare believe I'd hear ever again, especially tonight. "Peter!"

Standing a safe distance away, he glances around before he leaves the bushes and comes to me. "You changed your mind?" There's a joyful smile in his voice.

"Oh, I so hoped you'd come ba—"

"Good evening, Peter," someone cuts him off from behind me. I don't have to look to know who it is. If I survive this frightening adventure, I know his voice will haunt me for the rest of my life.

Peter stops dead and stares over my shoulder. "Hook." When his gaze moves back to mine, there's pain beneath a thick layer of anger. "You led him out here?" he whispers, hurt, but a moment later he yells at me with pure venom in his voice. "You allied with my enemy and freakin' brought him *out here*?"

"I'm so sorry. I didn't mean to—" How can I possibly explain? And suddenly I realize my mistake. Peter is so baffled to see me with Hook that he doesn't pay attention to what's really going on. "Peter! Watch out!" I scream, but it's already too late. Smee and two others ambush Peter, force him to the ground and hold him down flat on his stomach.

He fights and struggles, but not even his flying ability can help him against three men. Hook steps around me and squats in front of a cursing Peter. "See, little brother, I told you one day I'd get you."

I suck in a startled breath. That was no joke Hook made this afternoon? They really *are* brothers?

"And now I suggest you show me the way to my treasure or your friends are going to find you without your head in the morning."

"Shove off, you bilge rats!" Peter yells at the pirates, ignoring Hook, and starts to writhe under them again.

I run to his aid, but rough hands hold me back by my shoulders. Trapped, I watch helplessly as Hook grabs Peter's face with clawed fingers and forces him to look up. "Surrender and I'll go easy on you, little brother. Just tell me where the gold and the chest are," he says with barely leashed anger.

Peter's laugh is a painful sound. "When have you ever gone easy on me? You didn't back then, and you won't now." Smee is pushing his knee harder into Peter's spine. Peter coughs. "You want the chest? Go to the edge of the volcano and jump in. Maybe you'll find it there, asshole." Peter stuns me when he proudly lifts his head and imitates the cry of an eagle.

Moments later, a swinging bundle ambushes Hook from the side and knocks him off his feet. More bird cries follow, but not from Peter. The Lost Boys swing into the clearing on lianas one by one, landing on their feet, ready for battle. Three of them attack Peter's capturers, the rest go at Hook. I'm glad to see they brought real swords and slingshots instead of the toys I saw in their home yesterday. This way, they might stand a chance against the pirates.

As soon as Peter is on his feet again, the battle takes a turn for the worse. He snarls that Hook is his to fight and they go down a dirty road with their battle. Both sides take jabs and slices, punches and kicks. My heart stops when Hook spins on his heels with a sword extended, but Peter flies out of the way just before he would have gotten decapitated.

It takes me several minutes to realize I'm alone. Unguarded. Stan engaged the pirate holding me before in a fight. This is my chance to flee. To get out of the jungle and find help…somewhere.

Taking a few deep breaths, I silently apologize to Peter for bringing this doom on him, then I turn around and run for my life. The cries of the battle fade behind me as I climb over roots and duck under broken branches. It's dark as hell and I feel my way rather than see where I'm going, but I know I have to get as far away from Hook and his men as I can.

Suddenly, the ground disappears beneath my feet.

A frightened shriek escapes my throat. Hysterically, I flail my arms, struggling to hold onto anything I can. Sliding down an earthy slope, I grab onto roots that stick out from the dirt and cling onto them for dear life. As I tilt my head up, I can't see much, only that it's at least six feet up to safety. What's beneath me, I don't want to know.

"Help!" I cry out. Why I do that, I have no idea. Peter hates me and the pirates don't freaking care whether I'm dead or alive. But it's all I can do, so I cry out again. "Help me, please!"

One side of the root comes loose and with another

panicky shriek I drop a couple more feet. A searing pain spreads in my fingers from my iron grip. I don't think I can hold on much longer.

James Hook

"What was that?" I hear Smee shout beside me. I don't know what he means, and I'm too busy parrying Peter's jabs to even care. A second later, I hear it, too. The desperate scream of a girl.

Trying not to get skewered as I cast a quick look around, I can't see our prisoner anywhere. "Where's Angel?" I shout to my men, who are battling with the Lost Boys. Whalefluke Walter should have taken care of her, but he's fighting against three of Peter's friends alongside Smee.

"Wait!" I yell at Peter who's going at my gorge with his sword that's really just a big knife.

"Why? Need a break, Hook? Did you pee your pants?"

I dodge his next blow, strike hard with my rapier and cut his upper arm. "No, but it sounds like your friend is in trouble," I growl.

Peter hesitates a second. He seems confused and

unsure what to do. Apart from the shouts of the men and boys around us, the jungle is silent. Apparently he decides to ignore my warning. He comes straight at me, flying the last bit, and throws me to the ground. Just then, I hear Angel's faint plea for help again.

Whatever happened to her, she sounds terrified. We're even in numbers here and, as much as I loathe to admit it, we might not come out of this fight as the winners. If I lose Angel too, I'll go back empty-handed tonight. And I cannot afford that.

Since Peter is still focused on me and not listening to what's happening in the distance, I throw a hard punch at his jaw which tosses him off of me. Thanks to his stupid ability to fly, he lands ten feet to the side.

Climbing to my feet with my sword still in my clenched fist, I dash in the direction from which Angel's scream last came.

"What? Now you're running away?" Peter shouts after me. I know he's following me through the underbrush. I can only hope he keeps to some code and doesn't spear me from behind. I would. Maybe.

"Angel!" I shout instead of answering Peter Pan. When there's no answer, I try it again, louder this time.

"I'm here! Please help me!"

She sounds terrified, but at least she's still alive. I fight my way through the jungle for a few more steps and stumble to a halt when I find myself at the edge of a huge hole in the ground. It's at least ten feet in diameter and so black inside that one can't make out anything.

Smee and the others sidle up to me. They must have stopped fighting when Peter and I did. "Fire," I tell Jack, who runs back and brings the torch, lighting it again. As he holds it into the hole, I can see Angel hanging onto a thin twig that stands out from the earth. Her feet dangle in the air. There's nothing she can use to climb up or even just stand on. And fifteen feet beneath her, sharpened branches jut out from the ground. If she loses her grip, she's going to get impaled in that vicious trap.

Furious, I snarl at Peter, "Damn, you had to make this impossible to escape from, didn't you?"

"It's the only way to keep vermin like you away," he spits back.

"Congrats. Now fly down and get her out."

Peter takes a small step back and crosses his arms over his chest, staring me straight in the eye. "Why should I?"

What the hell was wrong with this boy? I thought I was the ruthless one here. "Because she's your friend!" When that argument obviously hits a wall, I grab the first boy nearby in a bear-fur vest and press my blade to his throat. "And because I'm killing this one if you don't."

Clenching his jaw, Peter throws a narrow-eyed look to his other friends. They all retreat into the thicket of the jungle. My men immediately go after them, but I signal them to let the kids go. I don't care about the rest. I still have little Bear here to make my point clear.

"Let him go and I'll save her," Peter bargains with me in a dead-serious tone.

Sure, he's deeply hurt because he thinks Angel betrayed him, but I don't see why he hasn't already flown down and saved her. This isn't how I know my little brother. For the briefest moment, I think I understand what's wrong, but that thought is gone too fast to chase. There are other things to concentrate on now. Slowly, I lower my sword and ease my grip on the kid.

Peter nods toward the dark jungle and the guy walks away from me. Peter follows him.

"Wait!" I shout. "What about the girl?"

Looking over his shoulder, Peter says in the same cold voice as before, "She's your friend, not mine." Then he flies away. The kid in bear disguise stops and gazes back at the hole for a moment, as though he's considering climbing down himself and helping her out. But when the cry of an eagle sounds above the trees, he quickly spins around and disappears after the others.

The frightened whimpering at my feet tears me out of my confusion. I step forward and gaze down, meeting Angel's glistening eyes. We stare at each other for the length of a breath.

"Please, don't leave me here," she mouths.

I won't.

Clenching my jaw, I hunker down by the edge of the hole and test the ground.

"Cap'n!" Fin Flannigan shouts out. "What the hell are you doing?"

"Saving the girl."

Smee squats beside me. His voice is low and anxious. "There's nothing there to hold on to, James. If you slip, you'll fall to your death."

I consider his concern for a second then nod. "That's exactly why someone has to get her out of there."

Smee pushes a breath out through his nose, plants a heavy hand on my shoulder and tells me to wait. Then he rises to his feet and tugs a knife from his belt. He walks to a liana, cuts it off and hands it to me. "We'll pull you back up when you're ready." As if on a silent command, all the others take hold of the ropey vine.

Grateful for the possibility to come out of this alive, I wrap the liana around my fist and start to slide down to where Angel still hangs on to a tiny piece of a protruding root. When I'm at her side, I can see how she's shaking and her breathing is hitched. Her hands have gone white from her desperate grip.

I ease one arm around her waist and pull her into me. "I have you. You can let go now."

The chatter of her teeth is all that comes out of her mouth as she shakes her head. The girl is petrified, and I'm the one who put her in this situation. In a strange

ANNA KATMORE

way, it makes my chest ache for her. I almost tell her I'm sorry, but at the last moment I realize my mistake. "You have to let go of the root now. I'm going to get you out of here, Angel, but you have to trust me."

Shit, who am I fooling? I wouldn't trust myself if I were her. But in her dire situation, she doesn't have much of a choice. Still, it surprises me when she suddenly slings one arm around my neck, pressing her face against my shoulder.

"See, that wasn't so hard." I hold her tighter against me to give her a better sense of safety. The softness of her fragile body catches me unaware. It feels good to hold her. Slowly, the fingers of her other hand loosen and she wraps that arm around me, too. "All right...I won't let you fall. I promise." As if the word of a pirate counted for anything, I know. This time, however, I really mean it. "Get us out!" I shout up to Smee.

The men pull on a counting rhythm, slowly lifting us toward the edge of the hole. Angel is shaking so hard in my arms, I'm afraid of losing her. Holding on tight, I bring her up with me. Smee helps her over the edge and steadies her until I'm on my feet as well and can take over.

As soon as I touch her shoulders, though, she starts fighting me. Thrashing about, she croaks some unintelligible words. She probably wants to curse me to hell, but no real sound comes out of her throat.

Angel was a tough girl when I met her this

afternoon. Tonight, I broke her.

She swallows a few times then tries speaking again without success.

"Let me support you," I cut her off, noticing that the front of her shirt is shredded and bare skin flashes between the many gaps.

"No!" Frantically, she shakes her head, tears streaming down her dirt-smudged cheeks.

Until this very day, I never had to deal with tears in my life. They sort of scare me. "You're under shock and not capable of standing on your own legs. Let. Me. Support. You."

I cup her elbows, which she thanks me for with a look full of loathing and a weak punch against my shoulder. "Le' go." Twisting out of my hold, the silly girl staggers a couple of steps away then tips lifelessly to the side.

I dart forward and catch her, sweeping her up in my arms. The cinnamon smell of her hair creeps into my nostrils. She weighs nothing, probably only had that one stupid apple to eat all day. She must have been starving by the time I made her walk to the jungle with us. *Well done, James.* But then I never said I was good at taking care of things. I shouldn't have brought her on board the Jolly Roger. That's why pirate ships are run by men. Girls mean trouble. They are so...dependent.

Whirling around, I face the small part of the crew

that came with me tonight. They all look at me like I'm marked with scabies. "What?" I bark.

Smee narrows his eyes. "What are you going to do with her?"

Yeah, that is a quality question. I shrug because I have no freaking idea.

Chapter 7

My head hurts and hunger has my stomach in a rebelling twist. Nausea creeps up my throat from a strange swaying sensation. Am I on the pirate ship again? I can hear quiet murmurs around me, but I feel too weak to open my eyes and find out where I am. Strong arms tighten around me and I realize I'm not on a ship. Somebody is carrying me. Hopefully, it's Peter flying me far away from Hook and his men.

I roll my head to the side, leaning my cheek against a warm chest. A familiar scent clings to it.

Tangerine and seawater.

No, no, no, not him! He's the enemy. I don't want to be here. I think of my happy place, my home back in London, and wait until sleep pulls me under once again.

A whispered conversation wakes me some time later, but I'm still too exhausted to fully come to.

"You want to take her to your quarters?"

"Well, she has to sleep *somewhere*, and the bilge is hardly the right place to put her, is it? But we can take her to *your* quarters, if that's a better idea."

"*No!* Your cabin is fine."

I'm placed on something soft. Blinking a few times, I can only make out the flickering light of a candle flame. Figures move like shadows in the room. My shoes come off and a blanket is draped over my body. The shivering fades from my bones. I curl into the soft pillow and reach out for my sisters in the dream that I haven't fully abandoned yet. Paulina laughs and flings her tiny arms around my neck. She kisses my cheek and tells me to come home. Closing my eyes, I do.

Something caresses my left cheek. It feels wonderfully soft. After a deep sigh of pleasure, I open my eyes and tilt my head to see what it is. The bright light of the morning sun flows through three wide windows and covers half the room with a blanket of warmth. Long white curtains are dreamily drawn apart and tied to either side of the windows. If I didn't know better, I'd say I woke up in a palace.

Of course, I know where I truly am—held captive in a cabin on the ship of the meanest man in the world.

As I sit up in a sea of white sheets, every single bone in my body hurts, reminding me of the worst day of my life. I wince and rub my temples. The last thing I remember is trying to run away from Hook after he pulled me out of that hole. Why he did it is a puzzle to me. A random guess: he needs me for another gruesome plan of his. But how much value could I still have to him? After last night it must be obvious to everyone that Peter Pan doesn't care what becomes of me. Honestly, who can blame him? He must think of me as the worst traitor ever, even if it wasn't my intention or my fault that I led the pirates to his hideout. I feel bad for Peter and the Lost Boys.

Wondering if it's a good idea to get out of bed at all, I let my glance move through the room. The bed I lie on, the shelves on the wall, and the huge antique wardrobe, everything is made of the same chocolaty colored wood— even the small desk set against the wall adjacent to the windows.

There are three doors on three different walls. One is right next to the desk, one in the wall opposite the windows where the wardrobe also stands, and one is leading to a room behind me. Curiosity makes me climb out of the cozy bed eventually, but I don't get to explore any further, because a tray on the desk with a delicious-smelling breakfast pulls me in like a pile of presents under a Christmas tree.

There's a pot with warm milk, slices of roasted pork and cheese, buns, and a bowl of fruit. Sliding into the swivel chair that's made of the same wood as the rest of the furniture, I tuck in like a ravenous dog and within minutes inhale all the food, down to the last juicy red apple from the bowl. Who knows when I'll get to eat again in this place?

Thoroughly full, I rise and walk to the door opposite the windows where the shouts of men and bustling on deck drifts to me. A handwritten note sticks on the wood at eye level, which I didn't notice before.

Look left before you walk through this door.

Turning my head left, I find myself standing in front of a mirror that's as tall as I am. *Oh my God!* Instinctively, I cover my upper body with my arms because my t-shirt is torn to shreds. It must have happened in the jungle last night—when I slid down that dangerous slope. It would be a stupid idea to face the crew with my body exposed like this. On a second look, bright colors behind me catch my attention. I swirl around. Three dresses hang on the side of the wardrobe, each of them breathtakingly beautiful.

One is blood-red, made of velvet, with a tight corsage and a fussy skirt. It has long sleeves that end in a flowing soft cone. The second is pink, sleeveless, and like the first it's so long, I would step on the hem if I wore it without high heels. I pull the third dress from the hanger and hold it in front of my body, turning back to the mirror. The light blue dress barely reaches my ankles and has tight sleeves that end just above the elbows. The cut is a simple baby-doll style with a satin bow beneath the chest. It's gorgeous. And the best thing about it is, wherever I go in Neverland, I won't attract attention wearing it.

Carefully placing the dress on the bed, I pull off my torn shirt. There I spot from the corner of my eye another note, this one on the door next to the bed. It reads:

Bathroom

Cautiously, I open the door and peek inside. A toilet is at the back of the room and—Wow! There's no roof! Two buckets filled with water hang over an open space, a string attached to both of them. Interesting shower. I wonder if it's all right to use it. Discarding the rest of my dirty, torn clothes on the floor, I slip into the bathroom and step under the first bucket, pulling its string.

A curse escapes me through clenched teeth. The water gushing over me is arse-cold. Of course it would be; it's seawater. There's a bar of soap in a little basket attached to the wall. I rub it over my wet body. Foam builds and the smell of tangerine drifts to my nose. It dawns on me that when I'm done in here, I'll smell like the captain of this ship. Well, nothing can change that now. Pulling the second string, I wash the foam off and watch the suds run together in a narrow gutter in the floor. The drain leads through a small hole in the wall and out of the ship, down into the sea.

There's nothing to towel myself dry with, so I pull the dress on over my wet body, which is difficult, but I manage. My shirt and jeans aren't good to wear anymore, so I stuff them into the bin under the desk, but not before I peel my travelcard out of the pocket. The paper card suffered a great deal when I jumped overboard yesterday. The dates are blurred, the corners creased, but the word *London* is still legible.

Tracing it with my finger, I let go of a heavy sigh. Mom and Dad will be worried sick about me. They've probably gone to the police by now and reported me missing. I wish I could tell them where to look for me. I wish I could let them know I'm still alive.

Good heavens, I wish I could remember their faces!

Startled, I sink onto the mattress. How can one not remember their parents? This is impossible. They've been there my entire life. We walked in and out of the same house for nearly eighteen years. How could I forget?

But the more I try to recall their faces from my memory, the clearer it becomes that this isn't all that has gotten lost. I don't remember their names, their voices, or even one single moment in my life we spent together. It's like they haven't existed at all.

What scares me most about it is that I don't even feel sorrow about their loss. I'm sure I should miss them, grieve because I'm so far away from them. But I don't. The words *mom* and *dad* have become empty shells in my mind.

Panic squeezes my chest. How long until I forget everything about my past? How many more days can I treasure the memory of Paulina and Brittney Renae? How long until I completely forget where I come from, what our house looks like, and who I really am?

This must not happen!

I'll do anything to leave Neverland. If there's a way home, I'm going to find it. I press the tiny card to my heart and promise myself that I won't give up. I will fight for whatever memory I can save and I *will* find a way back to my sisters.

Filled with a new surge of hope and determination, I rise from the bed and tuck the travelcard into a side-pocket I discovered in the dress. It's time to find out where we are—if the ship is still close to the shore and another attempt of escape makes sense, or if we're far out again, surrounded by a school of sharks.

My tennis shoes don't match the babydoll dress and they don't fit into this epoch either. The floorboards are warm enough, so it should be all right to walk out barefoot. The doorknob already in my hand, however, I hesitate as another note attached to the third door to my left catches my eye. This one is fixed with a dagger.

Do not enter!

No sound comes from behind this door. I wonder what's in there. Another treasure? Weapons? Someone else's bedroom? Tapping my fingers gently on the wood, I wait for an answer. Nothing. Not even when I knock louder. If there are swords or even pistols behind that door, it would aid in my chances of getting off the ship. Nothing makes a point like a gun in your hand.

Carefully, I turn the knob and open the door just a crack. After the first glimpse, my heart sinks. This is not a weapon stash. It's a boring study. I step farther into the room and look around. The odor of rum hangs heavily in the air. There's a huge desk in front of the continuing row of windows, a map of Neverland on the wall, and another door opposite the windows, probably leading out on deck.

I'm just about to turn on my heel when this door opens and sharp blue eyes meet mine.

I must have startled Hook as much as he startled me, because he freezes in the doorway for a moment. Then he runs his hand through his windblown hair and comes striding across the room.

My first impulse is to scream and flee, jump out a window, but panic keeps me rooted to the spot. Hook brushes past me and peeks around the door as though he's checking for something. Right...if the dagger has fallen off and the note went missing.

I know it's still there, so I chew on my bottom lip until he stands in front of me again, arms folded. The sleeves of his white shirt are rolled up to his elbows and I can see the angry twitch of his biceps underneath. Only the bottom half of the shirt is buttoned. For the first time I can see the tiny golden key on a chain around his neck.

"I assume you can read?" he snarls into my face and I look up. Swallowing hard, I nod. "Then which part *exactly* didn't you understand?"

He's trying to intimidate me. And he's doing an excellent job. My heart drums a panicky rhythm. Last night, I saw what this man is capable of. What's the punishment for disobedience on the Jolly Roger? Certainly something painful.

"Are you going to whip me in front of the crew now?" I whisper.

"What? *No!*" He pauses and his eyebrows draw even deeper than the scowl he directed at me just a moment ago. "Why do you think I'd do that?"

Fear has clogged my throat. "Because you're a mean person...with an ugly soul." And telling him this just might have doubled the number of lashes I'll receive.

James Hook

The fear in Angel's eyes almost chokes me. I thought I had done some good for her by rescuing her from the trap, carrying her back when she was too exhausted to even open her eyes, and giving her the captain's cabin for the night. Obviously it wasn't enough.

"I'm not going to punish you," I say with some force in my voice to make her believe me.

Angel lowers her gaze to her naked feet. "Well, thank you then."

Thank you? What bullshit is that? I'm a pirate but God knows I never tortured a woman. "Listen, I know I went hard on you yesterday. Won't happen again. You don't have to be afraid of me."

Her eyes find mine. There's a layer of confusion in her gaze and also a flash of hope. She clasps her hands in front of her stomach. "Am I still your prisoner?"

Theoretically she is, but I want her to feel comfortable, too. "You're my guest."

"Am I free to leave the ship?"

"Um…no."

"Then I *am* your prisoner." Sadness gives way to anger in her eyes as she walks past me back into my bedroom and closes the door. A click sounds from the lock when she turns the key.

My jaw drops. She freaking locked me out of my own cabin. I could walk out on deck and try the other door, but I'm sure she just locked that one, too.

She should have done that last night. Then I wouldn't have been tempted to stand by the door for hours and watch her sleep. And I would have never found out that she does know where the treasure is.

After Smee and I had taken Angel to my quarters and he'd left, I tried to drink myself senseless in my study, just to escape the urge to slip through the door and sniff her hair again, which smells so temptingly of cinnamon it intoxicated me all the way back from the jungle. I was down to my second bottle of rum when the soft sound of her voice carried through the wall. She was mumbling in her sleep. About her life, her home, people there, and how she longed to hear someone laugh again. Things that didn't make any sense to me. I think she even mentioned her real name, but I can't be sure and I didn't care much either. But when she started apologizing to Peter Pan for selling him out and assuring him that she didn't tell the *evil Captain Hook* where the treasure cave was, she had my attention.

She didn't reveal the location in her sleep, but now I'm sure that she does know where it is. I'm forced to keep her on board until I can tease the information out of her. And if she stays stubborn and I have to listen to her sleep-talking every night from now on...well, I know worse ways to spend a night.

But what she said about me—about my ugly soul—echoes in my mind like the beat of a drum. I realize I broke her spirit last night. Maybe I should try to repair some of it. She doesn't look like the sassy lass I met at the seaport anymore. And it kind of bothers me. If I can find my treasure with Angel's assistance, voluntary or not, I might as well help her find a way back to London in return.

"Smee!" I yell on the way out of my study. He stands behind the wheel steering the ship parallel to the coast, like I ordered him to do. "Drop anchor and get down here!"

Ten minutes later, Jack Smee meets me by the railing. "What's up, Cap'n?"

"I need you to run another errand."

A smug grin stretches his mouth. "More dresses for the girl?"

"No. The one she's wearing looks good enough." Much too good, I had the opportunity to find out while staring at her bare shoulders due to the wide-cut collar of the blue dress. "I want you to take a dinghy and two men. Go back to the port. Find every nautical map there is. Afterward go to the forest and meet the fairies."

"Remona and Bre'Shun?" There's an uncomfortable edge to his voice. I know he doesn't like talking to the fairy sisters. Nobody does. There are rumors they use young men for their obscure potions and charms. And then they can be...exhausting at times.

"If anyone knows something about this *London*, then it's them."

"So we're trying to help the girl now?" He takes on a huffish stance, arms folded, head tilted, and one eyebrow arched. "What about the original plan? To wait until she comes forth with the information we want?"

"Can't hurt to look into the maps in the meantime, can it?" I set my jaw to show him it's a bad idea to second-guess me, friends or not.

Of course, Jack isn't impressed by my harsh tone. Never has been. It doesn't help much that I've known him since I was six. On the other hand, it's exactly why this makes him the most loyal of all my crew.

"All right." He claps my shoulder. "Anything else?"

"Yes. Bring me a new hat," I grumble. "I lost mine in the battle last night and I feel naked without it."

Smee laughs. "I'll get you one with a bigger feather."

I watch him lower the dinghy with Fin Flannigan and Potato Ralph. It's a good thing the cook is going, too.

If he grabs some meat and fruits, we'll get something other than potatoes to eat for a change. The breakfast he'd prepared for Angel this morning was impressive. I didn't know we had half of the stuff on board.

Chapter 8

I don't know if Hook deliberately left the keys in the lock or simply forgot they were there, but it's nice to have the opportunity to retreat to a small place of safety on this ship. Since this is obviously the captain's bedroom, I wonder where he slept last night.

That incident with him half an hour ago in the study next door left me with a queasy feeling in my stomach. Ever since I put a foot onto this ship, he'd been trying to intimidate me. But last night, shortly before I must have been knocked out cold, he seemed different. Like there's a real human beneath all this ruthlessness of his. He didn't let me die in that hole, he gave me clothes when mine were torn, then he said I don't have to be afraid of him. What exactly does that mean? That he won't force me out onto the plank a second time?

Nestled against the headboard of the wide bed, my

legs drawn under the skirt of the dress, I rub my hands over my face and sigh into my palms. I've spent only two days in this crazy land, and I've already forgotten so much about my life.

Fear takes hold of me. I don't want to forget my past, so maybe I should start writing some kind of journal. Yeah, that's a great idea. But then, what if in the end I don't even remember why I wrote that particular story down? Or maybe I'll forget that it was me, who started this journal in the first place? Here in Neverland, everything seems possible and, all of a sudden, my stomach twists into a tight knot. Writing things down doesn't seem like the right way to deal with this.

Instead, I try to recall all I know in a mumble. "My name is Angel." Most likely. "I'm seventeen years old; I live in a beautiful two-story house just outside London; I like cinnamon cookies and strawberry milk, and my favorite movie is *Pirates of the Caribbean*." I stop and stare at my toes peeking out from under the skirt's hem. Now isn't this just ironic? I won't be able to watch that film without turning into a whining milquetoast in the future.

Okay, what else do I still know? "My sisters are twins, strawberry blond, and they love to make my life hell when my parents,"—the ones I don't remember—"are out of the house." Good. No important information has gone since I got up this morning. If I keep repeating these things to myself all day, I might not forget them after all.

And that's the exact moment a realization hits me. From morning till evening, I remember everything—all the time. What's there when I wake up is still there when I go to sleep. It's the time when I'm not awake where I seem to lose yet another part of my memory.

A shudder cold as ice pricks a trail down my spine.

Sleep is the answer. I must not fall asleep again, or I'll wake up with another chunk of memory lost forever. And that means I have to find a way off this island within the next sixteen to twenty hours.

Oh my God! *Don't panic now!*

I jump off the bed and pace the room. What options do I have? Neverland is a small island. The only chance to leave is to swim or board a ship. With the sharks out there, I opt for the latter. The passenger ships at the seaport are useless. They're rundown and have been converted to fit into a lazy town life. It would take weeks if not months to get them seaworthy.

Apparently, the only ship that still sails the ocean is the Jolly Roger. I need a plan to move the ship in the right direction.

Or...have it moved.

A wicked smile slips to my lips as I turn around and stare at the *Do not enter* note. It's been fastened to the door with a dagger. Heck, all the time it was there in front of my nose and I didn't see it! Seems like I don't need a pistol after all.

I pull the dagger out just in time to hear the sound of the other study door opening. The heels of Hook's boots clack on the wood. So he's back and apparently alone. This is my best bet to *convince* him of my intentions. I don't take another minute to think, just a moment to hide the silver dagger in the side pocket of my dress. It's too long and the tip of the blade stands out, so I cover it by sliding my hand into the pocket, too. With the other, I knock.

"Last time I saw you disappear into that room, *you* locked the door," comes Hook's muffled answering growl.

Right. I turn the key and take this as an invitation to enter.

Hook stands by the middle window behind his desk, his back turned to me. When I close the door, he looks over his shoulder. "What can I do for you?" There's a note of irritation in his voice.

I almost back out of my plan, but with the image of Paulina hugging her toy bunny in my mind, I take a deep breath, square my shoulders and say, "For one, you could let me off this ship, Captain."

Hook lets his attention glide outside again and chuckles. "Off this ship..." Then he slowly turns, skirts his desk and leans against the edge, his legs crossed at the ankles and his arms folded over his chest. Tilting his head and smiling just enough to make me wonder if he locked his nasty pirate manners away for a moment, he studies

ANNA KATMORE

me over the five-foot distance between us. "Tell me, Miss London, where would you go if I let you free?"

I shrug, lifting my chin. "Back to the seaport. Find someone who can tell me how to leave Neverland."

"You already know that this ship is your only way to leave. None of the people in town can help you. Most of them don't even realize that there's a place outside Neverland."

"But you do."

He loosens his arms and grips the edge of the desk with both hands. "I have seen others come here. But I've never seen one leave again."

I tighten my hold of the dagger's handle in my pocket for more courage. "Still, you think it's possible?"

A soft laugh rocks his chest. It's the same warm sound I heard from him yesterday before he lured me onto his ship. "Tell you what," he says. "You show me where my treasure is, and I'll tell you what I think."

My reticence yesterday on the edge of the plank obviously didn't convince him. "Why do you think I know anything?"

"Oh, just a feeling," he taunts me.

"A feeling?" I'm testing the word on my tongue. "Know what? I have a feeling, too."

"Wanna tell me about it?" Hook still looks like we're having a nice conversation here, while inside my body all my muscles are hard like taut wire. Admittedly, the friendly captain is much less disturbing than his alter ego. But I won't be deceived this time.

"Sure." I mimic his teasing smile. "I have this feeling that you're going to steer the ship away from the shore right about now and see if you can find London for me."

He lifts both his brows in a challenge. "And just what makes you so sure about that?"

Swiftly, I move forward. Pulling the dagger from my pocket, I press the point to the base of his throat. *There!* Stunned speechless, he stares at me wide-eyed and with his chin lifted. "My little friend here!" I snap. "Convinced?"

Amusement replaces his surprised expression and he starts to chuckle. "Not quite." Wrapping his hand around mine on the dagger, he moves it away from his throat. Simple as that.

My mouth falls open.

He straightens from the desk and steps closer. I don't have a chance to back away, because he's still holding my hand. My fingers would tremble if he wasn't pressing them together so firmly.

"Let me explain one thing to you, Angel," he says in a darker voice than before and dips his head so we're gazing at each other's eyes from only two inches away. "Never point a knife at a pirate, if you're not one hundred percent sure you'll use it." He brushes a strand of my hair out of my eyes and hooks it behind my ear, resting his hand in the crook of my neck and shoulder. "If you only had a little bit of the ruthlessness in you that you're trying to feign here, you would've already used the information about the treasure's lair to buy your freedom."

His breath smells of rum, but his eyes are sober. Did he just offer me a deal?

He starts to stroke the sensitive spot beneath my ear with his thumb and, all of a sudden, I find it hard to concentrate. His blue eyes look so much warmer than when I saw them the last time. Even though our foreheads don't touch, I can feel the tickling of his silky hair against my skin. Where is he going with this?

"I don't trust you," I whisper and try to blink myself free of his suddenly unbreakable spell.

"I know you don't," he whispers back.

"Where does that leave us?"

Slowly, Hook runs his tongue over his bottom lip, then one corner of his mouth curls up in a half-smile. "On a ship. Together. Trapped for eternity."

Jeez, he's teasing me. And he enjoys playing this game by his rules. But I'm not ready to play. I don't have *time* for it.

Backing away, I clear my throat and state more firmly, "You can't keep me a prisoner forever."

Hook tilts his head, amused. "Is this another feeling of yours telling you so?"

I want to scream "Screw you!" at his face, but instead I clench my teeth and snort at him. Then I turn away, needing a plan B and fast. It's better to return to my cabin. But Hook pulls me back by the hand I forgot he's still holding.

Carefully, he uncurls my fingers from the hilt while he holds my wrist with his other hand and says charmingly, "If you don't mind, I'll keep the dagger." He tucks it into his belt as he returns to his former place by the desk and folds his arms over his chest once more.

I just attempted to slice his throat open, and he's letting me go with a grin? What in the world has changed him so? With narrowed eyes, I look at him sideways, but there's no way I can figure him out. I let it be and stalk, chin high, back out the door. But before I can close it, I hear him call my name.

"What?" I snap over my shoulder.

"It's good to see I didn't break it all down."

Baffled, I turn once more and peek around the doorjamb. "All of what?" I say deliberately slow.

He gives me the first real smile. "Your spirit."

I open my mouth to say something then close it again. What does he care about my spirit? I shrug off my confusion and close the door, but without the bang I'd first planned on.

This encounter was even more disturbing than the first one this morning. His mood swings have me unsettled. Especially when they end with him caressing my skin. My stomach is still on a strange roll from that experience. I close my eyes and touch the side of my throat where his fingers were a minute ago. James Hook *is* an inscrutable man.

Unfortunately, he isn't willing to help me and I'm running out of time. So instead of thinking of his seawater-blue eyes invading mine, I should concentrate on finding a solution to my problem before the day is over and I lose more bits of memory to sleep.

Shouts from the decks give me an idea. Maybe I can bribe the crew into mutiny. But what do I have to offer to make this adventure appealing for the pirates? Nothing.

Well...nothing *here*. If I can convince the men to sail far out and find other places to plunder, they might show some interest.

With an excited grin pasted on my lips, I flit out through the door and take a twist in the warm sunlight. My glance travels over the wide decks. Where to start? There are four pirates by the lowest mast of the ship. They hold rum bottles and bark with laughter. Drunk and too many—not the best ones to start with.

To my right, I find the gold-toothed pirate who announced the captain on board yesterday. He sits shirtless on a barrel, cleaning one of his boots. Spitting onto the tip, he rubs it with a smudgy cloth. Gross. But he's the perfect member of the crew to tease into mutiny. He seems like someone who the others would listen to. Well, after Hook and Jack Smee.

As inconspicuously as a butterfly, I take a few swaying steps toward him, rock on the balls of my feet a few times and finally sit down on a heap of white linen and fishing nets. "Well, hello there," I say innocently enough, though I can hear how my voice trembles.

The man gives me a greedy sideways glance, but he doesn't return my greeting.

"What are you doing?"

"Cleanin' me boots, lass," he tells me in a rumbling deep voice and spits again. His saliva is tinted brown from tobacco and I have to take a deep breath in order not to puke.

"Is this all you do the entire day?"

"It's enough for now." Apparently he's done with this boot, because he puts it on and pulls off the other, starting the disgusting procedure anew. I watch, transfixed. "Why are ye so interested in me boots, lass?"

"Hm? Oh, I'm just wondering why you're spending time here, cleaning them, when you could be out doing, I don't know, pirate things?"

"Pirate things?" he repeats in an amused tone.

"You know like ransacking other ships...fighting with other pirates. Isn't this what you're supposed to do after all?" *Yeah, good tactic, Angel,* I encourage myself.

"We would. But the Jolly Roger is the only ship out on the sea." His eyes zero in on a spot of seagull poo on his boot and he gathers some real nasty phlegm from his throat. The sound raises goosebumps on my arms and makes my scalp prickle. He spits slime on the spot then polishes it off with the cloth. "There's not much to pilfer in these waters."

"That must be a boring life for you and the men on board then. I wonder why the captain doesn't let you sail farther out and have some real fun."

A soft laugh sounds from the sterncastle above. I tilt my head up and find Hook leaning casually against the railing on the bridge, obviously listening in on our conversation. He must know where I'm going with this and still he just laughs? I guess I'm safe then.

To show I don't care in the least that he's been eavesdropping, I flash a tightlipped grin back at him then return my attention to the shirtless man. "You should make him understand your needs as a pirate. What captain forces his crew to bob around a small island for years?"

"One who's after a treasure." When his boot is as shiny as can be, he slips it on again, stands up and shakes out the cloth. Only now I notice that it's actually a shirt. *His* shirt. And he puts it on. *Jeez!*

"Ye sound like ye don't approve of our cap'n's decisions," he states then and strokes his chin. "Are ye applying for the job yourself, lass?"

I stand up and shrug. "I'm just saying that pirates should be out doing *something*. Well, something other than cleaning decks or their shoes all day."

"A fine cap'n ye would make, pretty lass. All skinny 'n well-dressed." He gurgles a laugh and places his hands on my hips. Whoa, not how I planned this conversation to go. When he strokes his thumb across my cheek, I'm sure he leaves a trail of grease behind. I back away, but he wraps his arm around my waist and pulls me close. "All the men would be at your feet."

Suddenly he stiffens and it takes me only another heartbeat to realize why. The slim, sharp blade of a sword is pressed to his throat. "Take your hands off the lass, Brant Skyler," Hook tells the man with venom in his voice. "Now."

Mr. Skyler turns pale and jerks his hands away. "I was only jokin' with her, Cap'n."

"The joke is over. Leave her alone."

Immediately, the pirate scuttles off to the group of his rum-drinking friends. Hook throws them a warning glare over his shoulder, then he shouts so loud everyone on the ship turns and listens. "The girl is not to be touched! The next man who puts a finger on her is shark bait! Understand?"

There's a collective murmur of aye's from all sides.

With a tight grip on my upper arm, Hook drags me toward the stairs leading to the bridge. He didn't come down this way, I know because I'd been watching it. Did he just jump over the railing to come to my rescue?

Puzzled, I tilt my head to search his face. His eyes

gleam with irritation, surprise and amusement. I can't figure out which outweighs the others when he asks, "Why are you seducing my men, Angel?"

"I wasn't."

"Right. Unless I'm very much mistaken, you just tried to start a mutiny, which isn't very nice either."

For a brief moment, I stand on my toes to be on eye level with him. "Well, it backfired. Happy now?"

He pulls me closer until our noses touch and I gasp. "Do I look happy?" he growls.

No, he doesn't. But nor does he look as angry as he should be. In a caress-like gesture, he places the blade of his sword into the crook of my neck. I don't know what exactly he intends, but strangely enough it doesn't scare me.

"Are you going to slice my throat?" I tease him.

"No," he answers and even smiles a little. "But if you ever bother my men again, I'll be forced to lock you up in that cabin." With a brief nod in the direction of his bedroom, he makes his point clear.

I feel brave and smile back, not a fake one this time. "Fair enough."

"I'm glad we have an understanding." He eases the grip of my arm and sheathes his sword.

At the same time, a man in a basket kind of thing on top of the highest mast shouts, "Lower the ladder! The dinghy is back!"

I have no idea what a dinghy is, but soon I find out that Smee and a couple other pirates returned from a trip to the port in a tiny rowboat. They tie it to the ship and climb on board. Smee carries a bundle of long rolled papers under his arm. It must be something the captain has been waiting for, because his face lights up when he sees them.

"I brought the maps you wanted, Cap'n," Jack Smee exclaims and pats the paper rolls.

"In here," Hook orders and both men head into his quarters, closing the door behind them.

Maps? What maps? Could this be of any use to me, too? I tiptoe closer to hear what they are talking about through the door.

"These are all available nautical maps of the waters around Neverland," says Smee. "But Bre'Shun said to tell you, you won't find what you're looking for on them. She gave me this."

Hook laughs. "What did you have to give for it? Your firstborn?"

"Beaver meat," Smee grunts. "On every freaking solstice for the next five years."

They are talking in riddles. But then I can hear how paper unfolds and next Hook's voice drifts out. "A stellar map? Does the fairy think we'll find London in the stars?"

Did he say London? That's all it takes to switch off my reason and I burst into the room.

Hook, who's standing with his back to me, hands braced on the table in front of him, lets his head sink between his shoulders and sighs. "I realize that a note and a dagger on the door can't keep you out. But not even a knock this time?"

How does he know it's me?

Rooted to the spot, I fight my surprise, then I cross my arms over my chest and argue, "You were talking about London. I want to hear what it's all about." Waiting for him to turn around, I pray that his mood is still on the positive side.

He straightens and rolls up the map in front of him. "We'll take a look at this later," he tells Jack Smee, who nods and silently walks for the door. When Smee passes me, he quickly lifts his brow and whistles through his teeth once in awe, like he's dying to stay and watch what's going to happen in this room in just a minute. Only after the sound of the door closing, Hook turns to face me, his expression darker than a storm.

I gulp.

James Hook

This is a pirate ship, goddammit! Does this girl have no instinct of self preservation—or respect for the captain?

I take a couple of deep breaths to control my temper instead of taking Angel over the knee, which no man in this world could blame me for.

"You said I'm still your prisoner," Angel croaks. At least now she seems to realize she took one step too far this time.

"I did."

"And you refused to set sail and help me get home."

I mirror her closed-off composure, but with my arched eyebrow I dare her. "Did I?" My question silences her. She shifts her sweet lips to one side and narrows her eyes at me. "I merely refused to let you skewer me with my own dagger," I add...and smile.

Curiosity swamps over her face. "So you actually considered searching for London?"

Considered is the right word. "Aye." And I'm even

more inclined now that I know she holds information that I could coax out of her with the right tactic. Threatening her with death didn't work. Blackmailing her with the prospect of eternal prison on this ship only encouraged her to incite my crew to mutiny. Bargaining is something I loathe to do, but it's my last resort. This girl's will is like a freaking fort.

A fort I almost took over last night. And I felt terrible at that moment. Not something that happens often in my life. Maybe because I don't usually have to deal with troubles of her kind. Maybe...it's about time to send this little angel home.

Angel tilts her head slightly to study me from the corner of her eye. "I thought you intended to keep me on this ship forever? Or at least until you found what you're looking for?"

"I changed my mind."

Considering my words, Angel rubs her bottom lip between her thumb and forefinger. Damn, I could watch her do this for an entire day. How could I not notice from the start what a beautiful girl she actually is? The self-destructive urge to walk over and touch her soft skin again rises inside me and crawls to my fingertips. I lean back and clasp the edge of the table.

"And now you're helping me why?" she asks.

"To get rid of you."

Surprise swells in her eyes. Or it could be I just hurt

her pride. "Well, Captain, there's an easier way to achieve that."

"Really?" I tease her.

"You're a pirate. You could just kill me," she snaps.

"Don't be ridiculous. I don't kill women."

"Oh, sure." She takes a brave step toward me, lifting her chin, which she always does when she's trying to get the best of me. So much I've learned. "May I remind you that you would have let me walk the plank just to get some information out of me?"

"Yeah, and we know how well that plan worked, right?" I laugh and lower my gaze to hers. Now that she's a lot closer, I can even smell my soap on her.

Placing her fists on her hips, she counters with an edge of reproach in her voice, "You threatened to slice my throat because I called you *Jamie*."

And I had good reason for that, for shit's sake! I stand and close the last bit of distance between us, picking up her tone. "Because you undermined my authority in front of the crew! Someone had to teach you manners."

"Manners? And that from a pirate's mouth!" She rolls her eyes at me. Shit, that *is* sexy. "Was it also part of the lesson to let me lead the way through a labyrinth of deadly traps?"

"I was sure you knew where they were," I defend myself equally loud against her shouting, crossing my arms over my chest.

Angel lifts to her tiptoes so her face is almost in mine as she screams, "I. Fell. Into one!"

"And I. Freaking. Pulled you out of it! I saved your life, for Christ's sake! Is that nothing to you?"

"Hah, you've gotta be kidding! Trying to turn the tables on me for not being thankful now, are you?" The skirt of her dress sways angrily as she spins on her heel and walks into my bedroom. I follow her, but in the doorway she turns and shouts, "You're such an *honorable* man, Captain Hook!" Then she slams the door in my face.

What. The hell. Was that?

I'm the captain of this ship. No one is slamming doors at me or locking me out of my own room. With a powerful thrust, I kick the door open and it knocks into the wall behind with a loud bang. The lock is broken. Splinters of the wood skitter on the floor toward Angel's bare feet.

She whirls about, her cheeks heated from our argument, her eyes wide open. She looks at me like I've just offered her toadstools for dinner. "Why are you damaging your ship, Captain? The door wasn't locked!"

I already opened my mouth to reply, but suddenly I feel stupid. Standing in the broken door, I turn on the spot then back at her. Not locked? I'm such a fool. And what in the world made me lose it like that anyway? All I wanted was to make her see that I never intended to really let her die—on the plank or elsewhere. But this girl does grate on a certain nerve within me. "That is your fault."

Angel lifts her hands sideways. "Oh, please, enlighten me why *you* destroying the ship is *my* fault!"

"Because you just don't want to understand!"

"Understand what?"

"That I'm—" Cutting myself off, I fist my hands at my sides. This is hard. I press my lips together, holding back the words building inside me like a dam about to break. "Sorry!" I finally spit out and stalk away.

With the door providing no barrier any longer, even my quarters feel unsafe. Not looking back at Angel, I stride out on deck and pull in a lungful of briny air.

Finding Smee at the ship's bow, I grab his arm and lead him away from Fin and Black Death Willie. By the old cannon in the middle of the ship, I stop and face him.

"You look a little windblown," Smee mocks me. "Did you and the lass have a nice chat?"

I have no time for this shit. "We have to move her."

Smee lifts both his brows.

"Out of my quarters," I explain. "She's a distraction I don't care for."

Smee barks a throaty laugh at the hint of panic in my voice. "But how will you listen in on her when she sleeps, if you aren't next door?"

I already thought about that on the way out here. "We'll have a man posted outside her cabin at all times."

"And where do you want to put her?"

Good question. In fact, I haven't thought that far. All the cabins on board are occupied. We'll have to evict a member of the crew. "Someone has to leave the ship for a while. Who of the men have gone the longest without shore leave?"

Deliberating for a moment, Smee flashes a *you-won't-like-this* grin. "Well...that would be me."

Sending my best man away when I need him the most is not an option. He can leave when everything is sorted out—when I'm in possession of my treasure again, and when we've sent Angel safely home. Maybe. "Not happening, lad. You stay and help me through this." I give him a warning glare so he knows I mean business. "What about B. B. Radley?"

"Barnacle Breath? He's the only one who's really doing some work on this ship. If you must dispose of any of the men, I'd say send Scowlin' Scabb. He does nothing but drink up all the rum on board and nap in the bilge."

I sweep the decks with a glance and find the bilge rat soon enough with a half-empty bottle of rum tucked under his arm. He's sleeping away the day on the spare sail in a corner. I stroke the stubble on my chin. "You're right. And since he hardly sleeps in his cabin, it probably doesn't stink like the rest. I'll break the news to him, you find fresh sheets on this godforsaken ship and have someone prepare Scabb's quarters for a lady."

"Aye." Smee nods and in real pirate manner barks

orders to the others. At least there's still some normality on this ship.

It's hard enough to wake the drunken pirate with burn marks disgracing most of the left side of his face and throat—something that happened before he was hired as a pirate on the Jolly Roger. Once I don't have to grab his shoulders to support him anymore and he focuses on me instead of rolling his eyes from side to side, I tell him to take an extended vacation on land. The look on his face is hilarious. Like someone gave him a birthday present for the first time in his life. Not something that will ever happen, I believe. To anyone of the crew.

After that is settled and Scabb has taken off to the shore in the dinghy, I climb the steps to the bridge and watch Smee leading Angel across the main deck to her new quarters. I don't know what the men did to convert a pirate's hole into something that meets the tastes of a lass, but when she's popping her head back out after a short inspection, there's a smile pasted on her face.

Heck, did Smee put some goddamned daisies in a pot? When he glances my way, I beckon him with a nod. He says something to Angel then heads over here. In the meantime, I get the maps from my study and spread them on a table close to the wheel.

"There's nothing marked on any of these maps that looks halfway like another island," I tell Smee. "Neverland seems to be the only one in these waters."

"But we already knew that, didn't we? I mean, since that thing with Peter Pan happened, no other ship has been seen, no land discovered. Why would that change now, only because another lost kid showed up?"

I lift my head to look at Smee, but I don't really see him right now. In my mind, the image of Angel in my study comes up. "She's not just another kid," I murmur. "For one, she's older than all the others who've ever come here. And two, she didn't remain with Peter Pan."

"So what?"

My eyes focus. "Everything is pointing to the fact that she has come here accidentally. So if that's possible, it should also be possible to send her back."

"James?"

I arch my brows, waiting.

"You care for the lass."

"No, I don't." I'm a pirate. I can lie like that and no doom will come over my soul.

Smee purses his lips. He's a pirate, too, and of course he knows when another is lying. I don't give a damn, and obviously neither does he. "Fine. Then tell me why we're more interested in finding *London* than finding the treasure?"

"Angel is stubborn. She won't tell us shit, that much you must have realized. So instead of just waiting and praying that she'll reveal something in her sleep, I'm going to bargain with her."

"You think if you find the right way to take her home, she'll tell you where the treasure is?"

"Aye. She doesn't believe that I'll help her *after* she tells me. This way I may convince her."

He contemplates my plan. "Let's say we really get away from Neverland. Do you think we can just return after we've dropped her off?"

I take a deep breath and try to look confident. "We'll have to take that risk."

Jack purses his lips. He doesn't like my idea. There's just one way to convince him. "Scared?" I ask and smirk. "What are you? A princess or a pirate?"

Rolling his eyes, he huffs and I know I just persuaded him. He braces himself on the table, so his face is in mine. "But if she *is* going to spill in her dreams—"

"—then we don't have to worry about London anymore." I grin. And so does Jack.

After Smee is gone, I study the maps for some time longer. There really is nothing on them. But what did the fairy want with a stellar card? It's not like we have any chance to move out *there*.

Still, a look can't hurt. The map is in my quarters. I turn around and, just as I want to head off toward the stairs, I nearly bounce into Angel.

"For hell's sake, lass, can't I take a single step on this ship today without finding you behind me?" I growl and back away.

Angel stays where she is. Her hands are clasped behind her back and she still wears a shadow of that smile I saw on her from a distance. She's rocking on the balls of her feet like she did when she cornered Yarrin' Brant Skyler this morning. I get a bad feeling.

"The bridge is the captain's domain. What are you doing up here?" I ask.

"Umm..." She chews on her bottom lip. "I wanted to say thank you."

That is a surprise indeed. "What for?"

"Well, for a bedroom with a functioning door for instance." She pauses and the sunlight reflects in her brown eyes as they focus on mine. "And also for pulling me out of that trap last night."

"You're welcome." *You're welcome?* Son of a Biscuit Eater, what has become of me?

She cuts a look over my shoulder. "So you're doing this because you're sorry." It's not a question, it's a calm statement.

"Partly," I admit with reluctance.

"Partly...is...*good.*" It looks like she wants to smile, but it comes more out as a shy grimace. "What's the other reason?"

Now is as good a time as any to discuss this with her, so I tilt my head and say, "A bargain."

"With me?"

"Aye. You said you don't trust me—which I

understand. So I'm trying to give you a reason." When Angel seems rooted to the spot and nothing comes out of her mouth, I walk toward her with slow steps, knowing what effect it'll have on her. And I'm right. She's backing off one step for each of mine. "I'll take you home, and when we're there, you tell me where my treasure is."

We reach the top of the stairs and, holding on to the handrails on either side, Angel starts to descend them backward with me still following her, our gazes looked at all times.

"Deal?" I demand. She flashes a grin at me that reaches from one ear to the other. Seems like we have an agreement. I grip the handrails like she does. She takes one step down; I follow. "I want you to understand, however, that I will only let you get off this ship *after* you've told me."

She nods. "Will you start the journey today?"

"No."

Her abrupt stop on the stairs catches me unawares and I unintentionally slide my hands over hers on the rails. They are warm, but not as warm as mine. And they are fragile, just like the rest of her. She shakes a little when I wrap my fingers around hers and peel her hands off the rail. I don't know why, but it makes me want to pull her to me. Instead I bring our hands together between us and make her retreat farther until we stand on deck. "We're going to sail tomorrow at dawn."

"At dawn…" Her face falls as she whispers the words.

I think I've lost her. Sure, she longs to go home, but she's already been through so much. A few more hours shouldn't defeat her like this. On a strange instinct, I cup her chin and lift it to find her gaze again. "Why is that too late for you?"

Angel hesitates a long moment. Too long. It's obvious she's trying to shut me out. That's my fault and it should be okay. But it bothers me. A helluva lot. "Hmm?" I prompt her again.

"Because—" She sighs and steps away from me, pivoting to the horizon. "Because I might no longer know who I am tomorrow."

I don't know what it must feel like to forget basic facts of your life. But the look she gave me just before she turned away stabbed a part of me awake that most people probably call compassion. In pirate terms it's also known as the one little space inside a man that's responsible for the worst kind of trouble. If you don't have it under control, it makes you weak. And I'm just about to give control of this part of me to a strange young woman. I must have taken one blow too many on my head last night.

"Smee!" I yell over my shoulder.

"Aye?"

"Have the crew pull the anchor. We're setting sail."

Angel spins around to me, steadying herself on the

ship's railing behind her with both hands. Her surge of surprise and excitement is almost tangible. "We're going?"

With compressed lips I give a reluctant nod.

"I really misjudged you, Captain." Her honest smile is thrilling. On the railing her hands tighten. I have a feeling it wouldn't have taken much more for her to fling her arms happily around my neck. What did I do wrong that kept her from going through with it? "I can only hope you're not fooling me again," she adds in a calmer voice.

Like I've had the pleasure of finding out earlier this morning, her smile tends to infect me like the pox. This is a battle I won't win; my lips curl up and I lift one hand. "We will take you home, Angel. I give you my word as a pirate." With this I should be safe.

Her hands slip away from the railing. She takes a shy step forward. There, almost. I can already feel the warmth of her body. Her fingers come up. She's going to touch me in a second, and it shocks me how much I anticipate it. But then she retreats without warning and asks in a softer tone, "Mind giving me your word as just *Jamie*?"

Savvy, this one. Although I feel my shoulders sinking because she widened the distance between us, I chuckle. Then I lift my hand again and promise, "You have my word as *just Jamie*." Behind my back I cross the fingers of my other hand, just in case.

Chapter 9

The sun dips into the horizon. We've been sailing straight toward it for hours and hours. There's still no land in sight. I didn't move away from the railing for one minute. The bustling around me on deck has ceased. Several of the sailors have retreated to their quarters and some have gone under deck to end the day on rum. I'm almost alone out here. But not quite.

I feel his gaze on me. Although Hook didn't speak to me after the Jolly Roger set sail for London, he was watching me most of the day. I think it was on his orders that the slim and tall Potato Ralph brought me a sandwich and an apple for dinner.

At the beginning of our journey, I nervously ran up and down the long side of the ship. I was sure, once we just set course to *try*, we would find London soon. Now, as the day grows dimmer and night creeps in, chasing away the warmth, I just sit on a pile of wooden boxes, hug my knees to my chest and stare into the distance.

I don't want to give in to sleep. But I know in only a few hours I'll be so tired my eyes will fall shut. And when that happens, more moments of my past will disappear. I miss Paulina's loving embraces and the fairy bug's magic wand in my face every other minute. I smile at the memory, because it's the only thing I can do not to start crying.

Closing the world out for a second, I rest my cheek on my knees. *I will find home.* When I open my eyes again, I meet James Hook's gaze from the sterncastle, where he stands behind the wheel. A long black cape is draped around his shoulders and he's wearing a feathered hat. I think this one is new. It looks cleaner than the other.

He's the only one out here with me. Is he scared I'll take a mad jump into the sea to escape him? His features are soft in the fading light. No, that's not the reason he stands up there. He watches over me...because he cares.

I think sometimes he doesn't believe he can be more than just a pirate. The way saying a simple word like *sorry* troubled him this morning proves me right. There's more beneath his ruthlessness. He tries to hide it. But sometimes it flashes through. And it shocks me as much as it seems to shock him. It makes him adorable, turning the cruel Captain Hook into *just Jamie.* I find I like Jamie. If that's a smart thing to do remains to be seen.

I look away and place my chin on my knees. The night presses on my shoulders. There are a few stars in the sky now instead of the sun. One of them shines brighter than all the others. I close my eyes and make a wish upon it.

Slow footsteps draw my attention but I don't look up. I already know who it is. The footsteps stop beside me. After a long moment I hear the rustle of fabric and something is being draped over my shoulders. It smells of tangerines. "Thank you," I say in a low voice, knowing he just gave me his cape.

His footsteps sound again and I think he's leaving me alone, but when I look up he's holding onto the net that's coming down from the mast above us and he hoists himself onto the railing. The feather on his hat is blowing in the wind, the waves splashing against the belly of the ship the only sound.

"Can I ask you something?" he says after a long time of just gazing at me.

"Mm."

"What's waiting for you in London?"

The fact that he wants to talk to me about my home tugs at the corners of my mouth. "Family," I tell him. "A warm home. School."

He nods, seeming to understand what those things mean to me. Full of longing, I drop my legs from the box

I'm sitting on to reach into my pocket. From it, I pull the travelcard. It's creased at the corners. Smoothing them out, I look at it for a long time.

Hook leans forward and takes the card from my hands.

"Hey," I protest. "Do you ever ask before taking something?"

"I'm a pirate." He gives me a look full of amusement from under his hat. "I steal things. I feel bad when asking for them."

I laugh. "Too bad you can't steal the information you want from me then. Must drive you crazy."

"It does," he replies with dead seriousness, but his eyes stay warm and friendly. Then he examines my card more closely. "What is this?"

"It's a ticket for transport. With that I can travel from my house to my school in London." I sigh. "It's the only thing I have left that reminds me of my home."

After some time, Hook gives me the card back and I slip it into my pocket. "What's it like? The town," he wants to know, and he sounds somewhat enthusiastic now. I wonder if he's trying to sway me into a better mood. If he is, it's working.

"Oh, you would love it," I tell him. "It's bustling with excitement. Quite like the Main Street at the seaport, but far, far bigger. Bigger houses, bigger streets. To get from one end to the other people drive cars or ride busses."

"Cars?"

"Yes. It's a sort of transportation. Like a coach but just without the horse. They are so fast you could go from the north to the south of Neverland in less than an hour." I pause. "You do know what a coach is, right?"

Hook laughs and nods. "I sure do, but I much prefer *her*." He pats the railing of the Jolly Roger. "Your cars sound extraordinary."

"They aren't the only cool things we have. There are airplanes—flying coaches. And we have computers. They're machines that write for you and do other stuff. You can send a letter to another person ten thousand miles way, and that person will get it just a second later. You can also talk to that person through a tiny thing we call a phone." I laugh at the thought of him trying to figure out how to work one. "And we have boxes where you can watch people act out stories. We call it television. It's like you have all those tiny people in there and just watch what they do all day." My eyes must shine with ecstasy by now. "You would be amazed."

Hook studies me silently for a half minute, then he says in a voice full of understanding, "It does sound like a fascinating world...Angelina McFarland."

Something flutters inside my chest and I sit straighter. "What did you just say?"

"I think that's your name, isn't it?"

"I—" My breaths come faster and I twist my hand to

stare at the fading word *Angel* on my forearm. It was short for... *Oh my word*, Paulina and Brittney Renae used to call me that all the time. "Yes." I look up at Hook who lets go of the net and slides down from the railing. "How do you know?"

He lowers by my side on the wooden box. Briefly, he brushes his knuckles over my cheekbone and smiles. "You speak in your sleep."

I don't even want to know how he found *that* out. And I don't think I should like it so much when he touches me. His hands are calloused, but his touch is always gentle—when he decides to be Jamie and not the pirate captain.

"Did you hear me say anything else?" I demand, hoping to learn more about what I've already forgotten.

Hook nods and one side of his mouth turns up. His eyes shine warmer. "You called me an evil pirate."

"Yeah, well, you were! *Are.*" I pause for a breath. "You can be. Sometimes."

He laughs at my stuttering. Then he purses his lips and searches my face for a moment. "What about now?"

"Now...you're different." I hug my knees tighter to myself. "If it wasn't for your hat that always makes you look a little dangerous, I would deem you a normal, actually quite nice guy."

"Ah, the hat." He lifts his chin and mocks me with a penetrating look. And then he surprises me with the weirdest thing he could do. He takes off his hat and puts it on my head. "Maybe it looks less dangerous on you."

The overbearing brim blocks my sight. I shove it up a little and find *Jamie* smiling at me. He rakes a hand through his flattened hair and tousles it. It makes him look so much younger. Sweeter. I can almost envision him being a guy from my school. Someone I'd meet on an ordinary day. Someone who'd catch my attention in an instant. Someone who might ask me out, if things were different.

And I would say yes.

We look into each other's eyes so long, it seems the ship, the sea, the night, just everything fades away into unimportance. The air around me heats up. Or it's just the cape that warms me and I start imagining things. But who wouldn't when suddenly the sole focus of a notorious pirate captain?

"Can I ask *you* something now?" I say after a while to break the silence between us.

"No, you won't get scabies from wearing my hat."

That makes me laugh out loud and the sound of it dances around us in the otherwise silent night. "I didn't think I would. But that isn't what I wanted to ask."

He smiles. "Go ahead then."

"Peter and the Lost Boys told me some strange things about you."

"That I was an ugly, mean and scary man." He winks

at me as he shoves my own words down my throat.

My cheeks heat uncomfortably. "Yeah, that and something else. They told me about a hook on your right arm. First I thought you had lost your hand in a fight and replaced it with a hook. Obviously they were wrong."

"Er...not quite." Jamie blinks slowly. After some hesitation, he opens the cufflink of his white shirt and shoves up the sleeve until even his shoulder is bare. Shifting forward, he lets me take a look at his upper arm.

Whoa, there is a hook. It runs from the top of his shoulder down to the middle of his biceps. A silver chain is slung through the eye and wound around his upper arm twice. "A tattoo," I whisper with awe and stroke the fascinating design with my fingertips. Jamie's skin prickles into goosebumps. I quickly look up at his face, but he seems to be alright with me touching him, so I lower my gaze and explore the rest. Below the hook tattoo, the Jolly Roger sways with lowered sails on a calm sea. Everything is in blue and gray shades of moonlight. It's beautiful. "Who drew this?"

"After Redeye Johnson tattooed every member of the crew, I determined he had gained enough experience, so I let him ink this on me."

"You were right about my tattoo. There really is a striking difference."

"M-hm." Jamie lets go of the sleeve and it slides back down to his elbow. He takes my hand and gently runs his thumb over the sticker on my skin. "Yours is fading away. Mine is forever."

I start to shake a little under his caress and I know he notices, but he doesn't let go of my hand. He only lifts his gaze to mine and captures me in the spell of his blue eyes. "I think a skull and crossbones tattoo would look good on your skin, too. It would make you a real pirate." He sounds seductive. And dangerous. The only suitable combination for a man like him.

"A tattoo on my skin? Where would you put it?" I breathe, feeling a risky surge of recklessness.

He smirks and lifts my arm, inside up, to his mouth. "One good place would be here." With our gazes still locked, he places a chaste kiss on my wrist.

A shiver races through my body. The man who kidnapped me to his ship, the very one who almost had me killed in the jungle last night, is now gently breaking through my lines of reserve.

On a seductively slow blink, he lowers his gaze to my forearm in front of him and kisses the tender spot right beneath my elbow. "Or here..." he says and looks back at me.

My heart is tap dancing. I cannot move, cannot pull my arm away. I can't do anything but feel his caress...and enjoy it.

When Jamie doesn't move for an immeasurable moment, I think he's done. But I should have known better. He was just gauging my reaction. Leaning in closer, he reaches up and carefully slides his fingertips under the cape's collar, slowly dragging it a couple inches aside. "I've seen women with nice tattoos here, too," he murmurs against my skin. His next kiss goes to the bare crook of my neck.

My hands start to sweat. I grip the seam of the cape tightly to stop them from trembling.

Jamie moves the collar back into place and instead takes off my hat as he runs his lips up my throat in a barely noticeable caress. He stops just behind my ear. I feel the brush of his mouth on that sensitive spot at every word he whispers. "We could do a sweet little hook in this place."

I know my breaths come much too fast as our cheeks touch. His stubble grates a little on my skin. All I can smell is tangerines. I melt.

Bracing himself with one hand behind me, he splays the fingers of his other hand on my cheek and hair. Gently, he tilts my face a little more his way and skims the tip of his nose across my cheekbone until we're eye to eye. I can barely breathe at this point. He looks ruthless; he looks endearing. He looks like he knows exactly what he wants right now. But he's waiting. And I think I know just why.

He's asking me for the kiss.

Being a true pirate, he could have just stolen one. But

tonight *Jamie* is with me and, as bad as it might make him feel to ask for something, he gives me a choice.

My answer to his unspoken question is a shy smile.

He smiles too at our silent understanding and then he closes the last three inches of distance between us. I shut my eyes.

As he touches his lips gently to mine, warm and cold shivers take turns down my spine. Reluctantly, I let go of the cape still clasped between my fingers and reach up to lay my hand over his heart. It is pounding just as hard as mine.

He kisses my top lip, then my bottom lip, and the third time he uses just a little more pressure to make me open my mouth and invite him in. His fingers move deeper into my hair, holding me. A cautious touch of his tongue to mine, then another. He starts stroking it in a slow spiraling slide.

I feel like I'm falling out of the sky again. I push my hands up over his chest to the back of his neck and cling onto him, like he's my lifeline. We share the same breath and it's amazing. Thrilling. I know who he is, but he kisses me as gently as if he'd never spent one day of his life as a pirate. It feels like this night belongs to us alone.

"Cap'n?"

Shock slams into me and in an instant we break apart at Jack Smee's call from behind the pile of boxes. "James!"

Alarmed, I sit up. But Jamie only gives me a slack smile and places his hat on my head again. He eases back against the big wooden box behind us, his feet dangling from the one we're sitting on, and laces his fingers over his stomach. "I'm here," he says loud enough for Smee to hear.

Clacking of boot heels draws nearer. "I saw the vacated helm and thought— *Blow me down!*" Jack Smee looks like he's been hit by a cannonball as I tilt my head up to him. His focus is on me as if he'd mistaken me for the captain. Understandable, with me wearing Jamie's hat and cape.

Utterly uncomfortable now, I turn to Jamie. He reassures me with his relaxed expression. Not in the least bothered at being caught, he switches his gaze to Smee. "What did you think?"

"Ugh..." Smee runs a hand through his shaggy hair. "I thought maybe you wanted me to take over the helm."

"It's okay. I secured it before I came down here."

Nothing throws Jamie off balance. He's cool with the situation, while I'm way too warm and shaky. I wish Smee had picked a different moment to come out here. A moment hours from now.

"You can stay with the others. I'll be up at the bridge in just another minute," Jamie informs Jack, who mumbles an *aye* in return. When he's gone, Jamie's entire focus is on me again. He reaches up and brushes his thumb over my cheek. "I do have to get back to the wheel, you know."

Unable to keep the disappointment out of my face, I nod, hating how he takes the warmth with him when his hand slips away from me. I follow him with my gaze as he stands up. He only takes one step away from me, and I already feel alone on the wide, deserted deck. Suddenly he turns around again and holds his hand out. I think he wants to claim his hat and cape, but he smiles down at me and says, "Would you like to come up?"

James Hook

I can't believe I'm standing here asking Angel to come with me to the sterncastle. But then a lot happened today that I can barely wrap my mind around. Kissing her is on the very top of that list.

Angel stares up at me with big dark eyes. *Is she coming or not?* Giving people choices is new to me and it makes me feel uncomfortable. I actually start to feel like an idiot because she isn't moving an inch. Slowly, my arm lowers, but just then she reaches out and places her delicate hand in mine.

I want to growl: *What the hell took you so long?* But instead I find myself doing what I've done most of today when near her. I smile.

She rises and lets me lead her to the narrow stairs. The cape barely reaches my boots when I wear it, but now it sweeps along the floorboards as it hangs from Angel's shoulders. I let her walk up first and the feather of my hat tickles my face while I fasten the cufflink of my right sleeve. A chuckle escapes me.

"What's so funny?" Angel asks, looking over her shoulder.

I struggle to keep my face straight. "You do make a mighty fine pirate, Angelina McFarland."

"Pirate? Only if I can be the captain." She sticks her tongue out at me and jogs up the last couple of steps.

"You want to be captain of the ship? Fine with me." Reaching for her hands, which obviously surprises her, I unlock the helm and wrap her fingers around the handles, securing mine over hers.

Caging her in between my arms wasn't a smart idea, because now I have this girl standing pressed to my front and all I can think of is kissing that delectable neck of hers.

"I can't see," she mumbles and laughs. The hat has dipped forward into her face and since her hands are locked under mine, she can't fix it. I take it off her and put it back in its rightful place. At least wearing the hat brings back some feeling of normality. Abandoning the pirate in me is exhausting at best. But, oddly enough, for Angel I try.

Angel seesaws the wheel a little and I let her so she can gain a feeling for it. "How do you know you're still on the right track when all around us there's only water?" she demands. "A horizon at all sides."

"We started off due east from Neverland." I explain

to her how to use the compass worked into the counter next to the helm and she's all ears. I never thought she would be interested in how to steer a ship. Finding out she actually is gives me a feeling of excitement. Dreaming of keeping her on board for a while longer is just too easy. "You always keep an eye on this needle"—I tap the glass of the compass—"and make sure it stays pointed at true north."

"I see. So what happens when I do this?" She freaking spins the wheel in a fast circle and the ship tips hard portside, catching me unawares—and certainly the rest of the crew under deck, too.

"Blow me down, *lass*! You can't do that!" Falling sideways, I hold on to the helm and the railing behind her for balance and steady myself just before I would have run her over.

As she swirls the helm in the opposite direction and the ship tips again, Angel shakes with laughter. "Why not?" She's really having fun doing this.

The cape slides from her shoulders and lands in a black puddle of fabric on the floorboards by her bare feet, taking away the last bit of piracy from her and changing her back into the beautiful girl she was when I met her. The sound of her heartfelt laughter fills my chest with an odd warmth that I want to keep there at all costs. I last felt it ten minutes ago when I kissed her. Before that...never. Standing behind her again, I place my hands over hers and bring the Jolly Roger back to her original course. "Now hold her still," I say in her ear.

"Aye, aye, Captain." She mocks me with a grin over her shoulder. What she obviously didn't reckon with is how close this brings her face to mine. It only takes one blink of an eye and I have her captured with my gaze. She doesn't turn away. Her lips slightly parted, she breathes a little faster.

I know it's a bad idea, but I can't resist. Slowly sliding my hands up her arms to her shoulders and then farther on down her sides, I want to feel her, hold her and explore every little bit of her. But most of all, I want to kiss her again. So with a gentle push to her hips, I make her turn around to me.

Her eyes seem shy and she places her hands against my chest. I don't know if this is a natural reaction to keep me at a distance. When her fingers dig into my shirt and she clasps the fabric, I realize she doesn't want to push me away after all.

I thrust my hands into her hair, skimming the strands out of her face, and stroke my thumbs over her cheekbones. Slowly dipping my head so my brow touches hers, I take in a deep breath through my nose, trying to catch her cinnamon scent again. But there's only a familiar note of tangerines. I never thought it would be this intoxicating to know that the same scent clings to both of us now.

Footsteps come hurriedly toward us. I know who this is and why, without looking up. Angel's bold maneuver on the wheel worried my first mate. Never letting go of the girl in front of me, I say loud enough for my voice to carry over the empty deck, "All is fine. Go away, Smee."

His laugh drifts up to us but, thank God, so do his retreating footsteps.

"That wasn't nice of you," Angel breathes against my lips.

What the heck— "I'm not going to let him interrupt this again." And then I tilt my head and take her mouth in a way I've wanted to do since she went for my throat with the dagger this morning.

I don't seduce her into surrender with soft kisses but demand entrance from the very first instant. Angel releases a soft moan that I catch with my mouth. It's the most thrilling sound I know and it makes the little hairs at the back of my neck bristle.

Our tongues slide against each other, tender and sweet, like two birds dancing in the sky. I move closer to Angel, trapping her between the helm and my body. This is what my pirate side feels best at. She can't escape from me and I revel in possessing her. Like a treasure to keep.

But on a subtle whisper from the back of my mind, the sweet memory of Angel *wanting* to be with me comes forth. The sensation of not forcing her but getting all of her nonetheless was intoxicating. I want to relive it. So I lay my hands around her tender body and make her twist with me. My back is now against the wheel, my legs placed firmly apart, and Angel stands between them. I'm playing with fire—she can kiss me now or she can turn away from me. It's her call.

A heartbeat passes, and she just stares into my eyes. She knows exactly why I did this. To watch the realization dawn in her eyes is exhilarating. Like a poker game where you bet all without knowing what's in your opponent's cards until the very end.

When it's Angel's turn to show her hand, she lifts to her toes and brushes the tip of her nose against mine. A saucy grin spreads her lips. "Must be hard for a pirate captain to give up control."

"You didn't really think I would have let you get away, did you?" I tease her, wrapping my arms tighter around her. Suddenly, the words take on a deeper meaning in my mind. There will come a time when I have to let her go. If this journey is successful, even sooner than later. The question is will I be pirate enough then to ignore what she wants and steal her back? Or will *just Jamie* keep his promise?

I don't want to think about this now, but it's too late. Angel notices my concerned look. "What's up?" she says in her soft voice.

"Nothing." I shake off my frown and go for a smile. The night is too beautiful to waste a single minute of it.

Angel is in my arms and I want to savor her for now. I dip my head forward to kiss her again.

This time Angel hears it first and she stiffens. "Someone's coming."

Standing rigid, I listen into the night. She's right. A set of footsteps comes closer.

"Do you think it's Smee again?" she whispers.

I shake my head. Over time I've learned to distinguish my men even by the sound of their boots on wood. "Fin and Brant Skyler."

And to prove me right, Skyler shouts, "Cap'n. You still on deck?"

I draw in a breath to answer, but Angel startles me and claps her hand over my mouth, shoving me with some girlish force away from the wheel and behind the storage room on the bridge. "No! The captain has gone to his quarters," she calls over her shoulder. Then she locks her bright eyes with mine and whispers quickly, "Is there another way off the bridge?"

Since she didn't take her hand off my mouth, I nod, starting to enjoy her dauntlessness. "The captain said you can take over the wheel now," she tells my men then and makes me move.

I can't help but smirk at her before I take her hand, bend to pick up my cape from the floor and pull her with me. We duck farther along the railing of the sterncastle to the back, where a ladder leads down starboard to the quarter deck. As the men ascend at the front, we leave at the back and sneak around the corner to the front again. I don't exactly know where Angel is headed, but when we pass my quarters, I open the door and drag her in.

"Why did we come here?" she hisses.

"You said I've gone to my quarters. That's what I'm doing." I close the door behind us and lean against it, watching her walk up to the window in the moonlight. It's too dark inside. I want to see her again, so I toss my cape and hat on the bed and light the candle on the small desk by the wall. The warm flame makes our shadows dance on the walls.

When Angel turns around, her face is in skeptical lines. "Last time I was in here you kicked the door to trash."

"If I remember it right, you came after me with a dagger first."

She starts to grin and I wonder if she too thinks that it all seems so very long ago. Not like it happened only this morning. The clock strikes eleven. She must be tired, but I'm not yet ready to let her retreat to her room. I want her to myself just a little bit longer. Maybe an hour, I tell myself. Then I'd be happy. But at the same time I get this feeling that an hour wouldn't even scratch it. Today I found out that I can't get enough of her smile and her sweet voice.

Sitting on the edge of the bed, I reach for her hand

and pull her to me. "What would you like to do?"

She doesn't let go of me, but her grip isn't as tight as it was before. "I'd love to stand by the window and wait for any land to appear in front of the ship." A deep sigh escapes her. "But it will only lull me to sleep and I can't afford to even snooze."

"Because you're afraid of forgetting more of your life."

"M-hm." Her fingers slip away from mine. She walks past me and climbs onto my bed. I follow her with my gaze. Fluffing up the pillow behind her, she leans against it with her legs drawn to her chest. "Would you mind helping me stay awake for a while longer?"

Oh, not in the least. I twist around and let a smirk slip.

"Tell me something about you," she adds and with it she tramples my hopes of getting kissed again. "Anything to keep me from falling asleep."

She looks so forlorn on my bed. Helpless but full of hope. Her trust in me makes me think and do weird things, so I stand up then, take her hand and pull her forward to squeeze in behind her with my legs spread around her. "I have a better idea," I say into her ear and make her lean back against my chest. "Why don't you tell me everything you're afraid of forgetting? That way, if you really do forget, I'll be like your memory and can tell you about it again."

Angel tilts her head to look up at me, her eyes huge with wonder. "Really?"

"Sure." I lace my fingers in front of her stomach and she puts her hands on top of mine. Such a simple thing and still it heats me like a bonfire at night. She lets me kiss her brow, then she nestles her head under my chin and begins to tell.

After some time, I feel like I know everything about this girl. How she grew up, what she likes to eat and wear—mostly men's clothes from what I got out of her story—how kids her age go to schools and take tests. And then of course everything about her home and her family. Or the part of her family she still remembers. Brittney Renae and Paulina. She described them in so much detail that I feel like I've carried them around as babies myself.

When her voice ceases to a mumble with longer breaks every now and then, I know she's about to fall asleep. It's past two o'clock in the morning. I don't think she'll be able to stay awake much longer, no matter how hard she tries. So instead of prompting her to tell me more like I did every time her voice became lower in the past half hour, I remain silent now and just stroke the side of her face until her breathing becomes slow and even.

For half an hour I stare at the clock on the wall and watch the minute hand move ever so slowly. If I fall asleep now and Angel starts speaking again, revealing the treasure's hiding place, I might miss it. But chances are she spoke so much this evening that nothing whatsoever will happen during the rest of the night anyway.

Angel shivers a little in my arms. Since we're sitting on the blanket, there's nothing to cover her with. At the end of the bed lies my cape, but it's too far away for me to reach it without moving Angel. And I don't want to do that, because I don't want to wake her. She deserves some rest.

There's not much I can do other than wrap my arms around her, covering her own arms to warm her. She sighs against my chest and nestles a little deeper. Smiling to myself, I close my eyes.

I'm the one who wakes first. It's morning and a rock bobs up and down in front of the cabin's windows. The ship has come to a standstill. My first thought is to jump out of bed and see where we are. But Angel is still sleeping peacefully on me. She turned to her front during the night and her cheek rests on my chest. Her body lifts and falls with her breaths.

Skimming my fingers gently through her hair to wake her, I look to the windows again. There's something weird about the rock outside. It's familiar. With a sense of doom, I suddenly realize where we are. We landed on the west side of Neverland. No London anywhere near.

My heart sinks for Angel. This is going to crush her.

And then I won't get the information I need.

Chapter 10

Somebody murmurs my name. The voice is gentle and matches the tender caress on my cheek. Stirring awake after a wonderful dream about home and introducing Captain Hook to my family, I open my eyes and look up at Jamie's face. He looks worried.

"What's up?" I ask, rubbing the sleep from my eyes and sitting back on my haunches between his straddled legs.

Jamie rises from the bed and walks over to the windows then faces me. "You won't like this."

Now I'm really alarmed. Pushing off the bed, I go after him. "What do you mean?" But then I see through the smudgy windowpane there's land outside. My heart starts to race. "We found another island? Do you think it's where I come from?"

Oh my God, my home might not be far away!

"Come on! Why are you standing stiff like a mast?" I bellow with excitement and drag him away from the window, but then I remember my shoes and let go of his hand. I find them under the table and sit on the floor to put them on. Beaming, I look up, but he still wears a dark expression of concern.

I stop tying my laces as an invisible hand chokes my throat. "What is it, Jamie?" I whisper.

A deep sigh rumbles from him. He reaches for my hand to pull me to my feet. "That isn't London outside. Or any other island."

My chest tightens. Breathing becomes harder. "What are you saying?"

"That we're anchored at Neverland again."

The gentle strokes of his fingers on the back of my hand do nothing to soothe my breaking heart. "Why?" I croak. But then I already know why. "You lied to me."

"What? *No.*"

"Yes, you did!" Loaded with anger, I yank my hand away. "You said you'd take me home, but all you did was sail out into the ocean and then back again during the night. You're a goddamned liar!" Spinning around, I run with untied shoelaces out of his room and across the decks. From the corner of my eye, I see the wide green isle that is Neverland. Jamie calls my name from behind. Tears choke me and I run faster.

When I reach my own cabin, I slip inside and lock

the door then flop on the bed. My tears escape faster as I cry into my pillow. Why did he do this to me? Why did he introduce me to the caring Jamie last night, when *Jamie* is nothing but an illusion? There's only Captain Hook, and he is a cruel man.

Worse, I know I lost more of my past in my sleep. Wiping the tears from my eyes, I sit up against the wall at one side of the bed and reach into my pocket. There's still this little card inside. The *travelcard*. I sniff and tenderly stroke the worn surface of the paper. It bears the name of my hometown. But *London* is a black hole in my memory now with a single white house standing in its middle. Smells, sounds, colors and feelings are still awake inside that house, but the world around it has crumbled away.

In another day or two, my life as I knew it might be swept completely off the surface of my mind. What is going to happen once I forget everything? Will I believe that I've lived in Neverland all my life? Will I stay on the Jolly Roger and become a pirate, or will I find a place to live in the small seaport?

Will I be happy not knowing that somewhere, in a different world, two girls are crying over my disappearance?

All these thoughts scare me. I rise from the narrow bed and cross the two steps to the small table in front of a single square window. Everything in this room is much smaller than the captain's quarters, but Smee managed to make it look cozy with the pink carpet rolled out on the floor—certainly a stolen good—and the purple bows which he'd used to tie the curtains aside. Yesterday I liked his creativity. Today it only reminds me of Brittney Renae, and I start crying again.

There's a rap on the door. I turn around but I don't answer.

Someone's knocking again then trying the knob. "Angel, open the door. Please."

"No!" I tell Hook. I don't want to face him after what he did to me. "Go away!"

"Dammit, Angel, open the door or I swear I'll break this one, too."

He sounds angry—like he means it. Wiping my nose with the back of my hand, I grip the travelcard tighter in my other. In hesitant steps, I walk across the room and open the door. Hook is not wearing his hat, that's the first thing I notice. The second is a map in his hand.

His hard expression changes to silent shock when he sees me. I don't know what it is that stuns him so, but in another moment the map slips from his hand and he reaches out for my face. Callused thumbs brush my tears away. "Please, don't do that," Jamie whispers and pulls me against his chest.

Honestly, I don't know how to stop my tears when my last bit of hope slipped away this morning. "I thought we had become more than just pirate and prisoner last night," I mumble into the fabric of his white shirt. The words hurt my tight throat. "I thought we had become friends. Why did you lie to me, Jamie?"

His muscles tense for a brief moment and he stops caressing my hair. "I don't know what we became last night," he says then and it sounds soft and honest. "But I didn't lie to you about this. To find we're back at Neverland was as great a shock to me as it was to you."

I look up at his face, sniffing. "Then what happened? Why are we back?"

Jamie wraps his fingers around my shoulders and pushes me a little away from him. "It's weird," he says. Then he leans down to pick up the map. "Basically, what happened is we started off here—" Holding the yellowed paper out so I can see Neverland in the middle of the ocean, he taps the east side of the island with his finger. Then he runs his finger in a horizontal line across the ocean while turning the map in a circle, finally tapping the west side of Neverland. "And we landed here."

"How is that possible?"

He shrugs. In his eyes I see the truth.

"It's over," I whisper. "I'll be stuck here forever." My heart feels like it's spiked with lances that stab me at every beat. Jamie drops his arm with the map and shapes his other hand to my cheek, clearly not knowing how to soothe me. "I don't want to stay here forever!" The words burst free from my throat. "I want to go home, Jamie. I want to go back to my family."

The sigh that escapes him sounds like his throat is aching as much as mine. It's hard to believe it from the man who acted like he didn't give a damn about my life only two days ago, but right now I can feel that he cares for me. Suddenly he abandons his forlorn look. In its place slips determination. "Come with me," he says and takes my hand.

"Where are we going?" I demand as he drags me across the deck. Moments later, he has Brant Skyler extend the gangplank so we can get on land. There's barely enough time for me to tie my shoelaces.

Although Jamie walks first, he doesn't let go of my hand. Instead he reaches back to steady me and looks over his shoulder every few seconds. "We're going to meet a fairy."

"A fairy—like a pixie?" I wonder if he's talking about Tami, but when I realize we're heading to the seaport and not toward the jungle, the thought vaporizes.

"No, not like a pixie. More like a nymph from the forest. Actually two of them."

"Is there a difference?"

Jamie gives me a sidelong glance, pursing his lips. "You'll see yourself."

"And why are we going to see them?"

"Because they are the only ones who can help you get home. If anyone can, that is."

I have trouble keeping up with his pace. He must believe there's a real chance. So much euphoria in his eyes is new to me. It gives me hope.

When we reach the small town, we don't walk down the main road but angle off left and soon reach a lush green forest with low trees, mushrooms and moss everywhere, and bunnies ducking under the bushes. I have to stop to catch my breath for a minute, twisting on the spot and taking in all of this fabulous scenery. It's more than just romantic. It's bewitching.

"I hope they're home," Jamie mumbles as I follow him over the grassy ground without any real path. The deeper we get into the forest, the taller and thicker the trees grow. They create a dusky atmosphere. Only specks of light get through the crowns and land like glinting coins on the ground. They tempt me to stoop over and try to pick them up.

Behind a group of conifers ahead, a low white picket fence comes into view. It winds around a small house with a roof made of a thick layer of thread rush. From the chimney, a thin line of smoke rises toward the sky.

"We're here," Jamie informs me, then he stops and makes me face him. Suddenly I get nervous. Maybe it's the lines of seriousness around his eyes that worry me. Cupping my chin, he produces a little smile. "You don't have to be scared. They are really nice women. But whatever you do, don't talk to Remona."

His last warning raises my hackles.

There's no time to ask questions. The low green door opens. My attention pastes onto the beautiful, tall woman who ducks through the doorframe, then straightens and lifts her long gown of cascading silk the color of pomegranate. She wears no shoes and still towers a few inches over Jamie when she nears us. Her lips shine in a glossy green that seems to be their natural color and blend in with her pale skin. Enchanting turquoise eyes flash when she smiles.

"James Hook," she drawls with a joyous sigh. "How long has it been since you last came to the forest?"

"A while," Jamie replies with guilt in his voice and lets the fairy place a chaste kiss on his cheek. "I was busy."

"I realize that. The time keeps standing still."

Even if I don't, Jamie obviously knows what she's talking about. Grimacing, he rubs his neck. "Yeah, I haven't found the watch yet. But I'm getting closer."

"There will be no tomorrow if you fail."

"I know," he murmurs. I'm dying to know what this is all about, but since I have no chance to tell if this is Remona or not, I don't dare ask. As if to distract the fairy from their current topic, he places a hand at the small of my back and pushes me a step forward. "This is my friend, Angelina. Angel, meet Bre'Shun." With a smile he encourages me to shake her hand.

The fairy's skin is cold like spring water. My fingers

start to numb within only a moment. She doesn't release me but steps closer and tilts her head to one side, while she searches my face.

"Angelina McFarland. It's a pleasure to meet you."

My mouth sags open. I cut a brief glance to Jamie, mouthing, "Did you—" But he shakes his head with quirked brows. Obviously he's as surprised as I am about the fairy knowing my full name.

Bre'Shun laughs. "I know many things, Angelina. For instance that you're a visitor and can't find your home."

"Smee told you," Jamie states.

"No." When she shakes her head, her long fair locks glisten like stardust in the pixel-like sunlight. "I told *him*."

Right. This is probably what you get when dealing with a fairy. I find her fascinating and am happy to follow when she invites us into her house. The arc of the door is so low that even I have to stoop when I walk through. From the neat, tiny outside, I expect to be crammed into a three-by-three-meter living room. But the inside is huge. In fact, it's bigger than huge. It's like someone fit a palace into a shoebox.

Turning around to check if we really walked through that door, I can see the open gate of the picket fence. "What the heck—" I whisper to Jamie, but he only shakes his head. He certainly knew what to expect in here. A warning would have been nice.

Bre'Shun lays her hand on my shoulder to steer me

toward a wide glass table in the middle of the hall. The contact with her skin again makes me shudder. This time the cold travels even faster through my body. I'm glad when she lets go and quickly rub the spot to warm it up again.

The walls in this empty hall are made of rocks fitted against each other. The floor is a marble chessboard of black and white tiles. Even though there are no windows, the inside is flooded with daylight. I can't explain to myself where that comes from.

Three medieval chairs with rosé-colored upholstery appear around the table. Jamie and I sit down at Bre'Shun's invitation. Out of thin air, a silver tray with three white porcelain cups and a round pot on it appears in her hands. She places it in the middle of the table and slowly lowers herself into the third chair. Immediately, one cup on a saucer zooms in front of each of us. Then she laces her fingers and tilts her head to Jamie with a warm smile. "What can you do for me?"

Her question takes me by surprise. That was surely just a slip of her tongue I decide and take a sip of my herbal tea, waiting for her to correct herself. But she doesn't. And then something strange happens in the corner of the hall which draws all my attention. A tall grandfather clock appears by the wall and strikes half past one.

Bre'Shun has noticed my fixated attention and gives

ANNA KATMORE

me an understanding nod. Either I missed the clock at the beginning, or something very weird is going on inside this house. I don't feel like asking her about this.

When the fairy's attention returns to Jamie, she places a hand on top of his and a shudder twitches through him. Obviously, he doesn't like the chilling sensation any more than I do. "Now, your offer?" she demands.

"The roof looks a little rundown from the outside. I can fix it."

"Oh, dear James. The answer you want is worth more than adding a layer of thread rush to our roof."

Jamie shrugs. "That and fresh seawater in bottles every morning? For...a year?"

Heck, now I get it. He's bargaining with her for an answer. And the question is...how can I leave Neverland? Impressed by the lengths to which he would go to help me, I tilt my head at him and study his face. He ignores me and takes a sip of his own tea. For a brief moment, his gaze zeroes in on something over Bre'Shun's shoulder, but I see nothing there.

"Nice try," the fairy tells him in a soft tone. "But it's not what I want from you."

Then what does she want? An odd conversation I eavesdropped on yesterday resurfaces in my mind. Hook asked Smee what he had to give the fairy for the map. His guess was Smee's firstborn. Yesterday I thought it was only a joke. Now I wonder if this is what the fairy could bribe out of Jamie for helping me.

Bre'Shun laughs. "No, not his firstborn, Angelina. We don't use babies for charms."

So it's ingredients she wants. Ashamed of my assumption, and even more ashamed that she could somehow hear my thoughts and voiced them in front of Jamie, too, I lower my head and take a second sip of the tea. Right then, another object appears next to the grandfather clock. A rocking chair. Immediately, I put the cup down and it clinks angrily on the saucer. What freaking sorcery is this?

I feel Jamie's curious stare on me and for some reason I know it's because of what I'd thought and not how weird I'm acting right now. I give him a sidelong glance and shrug, grimacing. He chuckles, which eases my tension eventually.

"I know you already have something in mind, Bre," he says to the fairy. "What is it?"

She studies him for a long moment, her expression unchanging but warm. "The bathwater of a toddler," she finally says. "After a new moon."

Holy cow, how could he ever bring her such a strange thing? He has to break into somebody's house to get it.

"Agreed."

I suck in a sharp breath at Jamie's response.

"Very well, James Hook. I take you by your word." Her eyes glimmer more blue than turquoise now as she takes his hand into hers once more. The soft smile that has been pasted on her lips since we got there disappears. She still looks friendly, but a lot more serious. "One can leave Neverland only in the same way they first arrived."

I'm waiting for more.

There is nothing more.

I realize I'm screwed.

When Jamie pulls his hand away from the fairy, it has already started to turn blue from the cold. "Why didn't you tell this to Jack when he came here yesterday?" he demands.

Someone giggles behind us and I jerk around in my chair. "You sent him with the wrong question," another woman just as beautiful as Bre'Shun tells him. Her smooth silvery hair is as long as Bre'Shun's and she twists one strand of it around her finger. This must be Remona. Her sleeveless silk dress clings to her like melting white chocolate.

"Of course." Jamie sighs, sounding like he regrets a vast mistake. Then he rises from his chair and places his hand on my shoulder. "It's time to go," he whispers down to me.

I stand, but suddenly a crazy urge rides me. What if I drank a little more of the tea? Would more objects appear?

Bre'Shun walks around the table toward us, saying

goodbye to Jamie. Only half listening to them, I catch her strange words. "You're on the edge of your biggest adventure, James Hook. Don't push it away." I can't make sense of it, and I'm more focused on the teacup anyway. Before I face the fairy, I quickly take another sip. A potted plant appears on a small round table next to the rocking chair.

This is amazing and it freaks me out. But I can't resist. I take another draught. A window appears and the hall starts to shrink. Another sip, there's a mantelpiece. Warm fire burns inside. I drink the rest of the tea. When I look up, three more windows have appeared, the room shrank to one third of the hall's original size, the floor tiles are gone, replaced by a purple carpet, and for all I can tell, we didn't sit by a glass table with high-back chairs, but on a low L-shaped couch with a wooden coffee table in front.

My mouth is hanging wide open. Bre'Shun steps up to me and takes both my hands into hers. "Welcome to my home, Angelina." Her skin doesn't feel as cold as before.

Gratefully, I squeeze her hands now and tell her thanks and goodbye. But when I turn away from her, I find Remona in my face. Her smile isn't the warm and welcoming sort, but of absolute intrigue. She runs her fingers through my hair, feels the fabric of my dress and even bends low to examine my shoes.

"Incredible! A real visitor! I've never met an outsider

before." She pulls my shoelaces open and holds one end in her hand. "Look at those, Bre. What would I give for a glimpse into her world."

I feel a little uncomfortable under her close inspection, also because Jamie's warning still rings in my ears.

"Do you like it here in Neverland?" she asks me, rising.

"I—er..." I clasp my hands and bend down to tie the shoelace she left dangling then I straighten again. "It's a really interesting island. But I'd rather go home."

"I see, I see." She flits around me and faces me once more with a broad grin. "Can I get you to bring me a pair of these next time you come?" She points at my shoes.

"Well, ye—"

"No!" Jamie shouts and squeezes himself between me and Remona. With his mouth lowered to my ear, he snarls, "Your word to a fairy is binding for life." I only have to look into his eyes to read what he means. If I'd said yes, I would have had to come back and bring her shoes, no matter what.

"We have to go now," he tells Remona over his shoulder and shoves me out the door.

"Wait! Let me open the garden gate for you," her excited offer comes from behind. And in the next instant I feel like someone dragged my body through ice-cold water. I shudder. A cough like it's my last breath escapes me. In front of us, Remona appears out of nothing and skips to the low gate. Or she might have appeared out of…me.

I clasp Jamie's arm, my expression horrified. "Did she just walk through me?" I breathe.

He nods and grimaces. I can't wait to get away from this place.

With his arm around my waist, Jamie leads me out of their neat garden and back the way we had come. After a few steps I stop and glance back. Bre'Shun is still standing in the doorway. Behind her, there's a glass table with three high-back chairs and a chessboard floor.

"James," she says on a soft drawl and smiles at him alone. "Your next question will be even bigger than this. When you come for the information, bring a rainbow. From Neverland's middle."

I feel how a surge of astonishment weakens Jamie's hold of me. His eyes are wide and he slowly runs his tongue over his lips. For all of ten seconds he just stares at her. Finally he says, "Until we meet again, fairy."

She nods and disappears into her house, closing the door.

James Hook

A freaking rainbow from the volcano? What could possibly become so important to me in the future that I must catch a rainbow for it? If it was any other person speaking to me, I'd answer with a smile and leave it at that. But this is Bre'Shun. The fairy. She's always right about her forecasts. A shudder trails down my back.

"Let's go," I tell Angel and make her move through the thick forest. She follows without hesitation.

"Did you notice there was something wrong with the tea?" she whispers after a while even though we're already half a mile away from the fairies' house.

I answer in a normal voice, "Yeah. I thought I saw things appear after drinking it, but I wasn't too sure it was the tea. One can never tell at their home."

"Do you see them often?"

"The fairy sisters? I haven't been there in years. There was no need to."

Angel looks over her shoulder as if to make sure

we're finally far enough away to relax. Then she pulls me to a stop and faces me. There are wrinkles of confusion on her brow. "Okay, now explain."

"Explain what?"

"What she meant with her cryptic answer. That I can only leave Neverland the way I arrived."

"You said you came to the island through the sky."

"I did. But you don't have aircrafts as far as I can tell. How can I leave through the sky again?"

I wonder what an aircraft is. Maybe it's one of those flying coaches she told me about last night. It certainly would be easier to get away with one of those than what lies ahead of Angel. I sigh. "Basically I think you have to learn to fly."

"Me? Fly?" Her voice booms through the woods. "You might have missed it, but I don't have freaking wings!"

"You don't need wings to fly. What you need is a teacher." I hate what I'm going to say next, but I don't see any way around it. "You have to learn to fly like Peter Pan."

All air whizzes out of her lungs and she goes pale. "I can't do this. I don't know how to. And even if there's a way for Peter to show me—he's mad at me. He *hates* me!"

Because Angel talks herself into a frenzy, I place my hands on her shoulders, trying to soothe her, but she doesn't focus even when her eyes are locked with mine.

"He would never agree, Jamie. But it doesn't matter, because I can't ask him. He lives in the jungle and there's no way I'd ever go back in *there*!"

"Angel. *Angel!*" I brush her hair off her forehead and fight for her attention. "You don't have to walk through the jungle again. I won't let you. We will just have to wait until Peter comes to us. He knows where we are. He'll find the ship easily."

"Are you crazy? Why would he come to the ship? Even if he gets bored one day and decides to go for a fun battle with you, it could take weeks. Months… *Years!*"

"With any luck, he'll show up in the next couple of days."

That silences her and for once she's focusing on me. "What in the world makes you think so?"

"I have a plan." Not a very good one and chances are it totally backfires, but after I saw Angel crying this morning, I'm ready to try a *whole damn lot* to help her find home. And it's the only chance I have to get to my treasure as well. "We're going to leave a message for him."

Skepticism mars her face. She takes a step away from me and folds her arms over her chest, pursing her lips. "Whatever telephone connection they use in the tree house, I'm sure they don't have voice mail."

She's from a different world; I don't have to make sense of everything she says.

"Peter is friends with the mermaids. If we can

convince them to deliver our message next time they see him, we might get lucky."

Angel deliberates over my plan, walking in small circles around me and rubbing her temples. "But what will you tell him? He won't agree to help me." Her eyes find mine. "You saw how he left me hanging in that deathly hole the other night. He doesn't care what happens to me."

I caress her heated cheek. "He left you hanging because he thought you'd betrayed him. Leave this to me." If I can make him listen, he'll understand. Hopefully...

I take Angel back to the Jolly Roger and have Smee set the sails. We're heading north to Mermaid Lagoon. Angel is anxious all the time and grows quieter by the minute. Potato Ralph brings her meat and bread, but she doesn't even glance at the food.

I didn't talk to her about London all day. Now that I see her biting her nails and staring out at the sea, I wonder how much she still remembers. Which bit left her memory while she slept? I want to walk to her, take her in my arms and assure her that it's going to be alright. That we'll find a way to make her fly. But the truth is she's right. Peter is a stubborn boy. If I want to sway him to help me, it will take more than a *pretty please* between brothers. The important question is how much am I willing to give to make Angel happy?

I also realize I haven't kissed her all day. I miss that.

ANNA KATMORE

At twilight, I help her climb down to the dinghy and row us to the shore. We're still more than a mile away from the lagoon, but chances are the mermaids will escape underwater if they see the Jolly Roger nearing. It's best we walk the last bit.

In the chilly air, I remove my cape and wrap it around Angel's shoulders, tying the strings at the collar. It's going to be dark soon, and I don't know how long we'll have to wait for a mermaid to show up. Maybe a couple of minutes, but it could also be a few hours. I don't want her to be cold while we're out.

She lifts her gaze to mine and murmurs, "Thank you."

Nodding, I take her hand and slide my fingers through hers. I've never walked like this with anybody. When I stroke her knuckles with my thumb, she squeezes my hand gently in return. It's thrilling on a level beyond measure. Deeply connected, I shudder from the pleasure of it. There's no way to deny it, I'm going to miss her when she's gone. The realization comes with a twinge of pain.

"What's up?" she demands as we near the rocky shore at Neverland's north peak.

I don't see where that question is coming from. "Hm?"

"You sighed. What's troubling you?"

Heck, I sighed? Then it's even worse than I thought. "It's nothing," I lie. "I'm just thinking about how to make this work. You better keep your fingers crossed that the mermaids don't run when they see me."

"Swim," she corrects me and cuts me a mocking sideways glance.

"Smart mouth."

Angel giggles. It's a heartwarming sound. "What's your biggest adventure?" she asks me moments later.

It seems I just can't follow her mental leaps tonight. "What do you mean?"

"Bre'Shun said something weird to you earlier. Apart from all the other strange stuff she said, that is."

We reach the land of dark rocks leading like a dock out into the sea. I take a wide step onto the first rock, then turn around and hold my hand out for Angel. When she stands safely in front of me again, she stares at my face and continues, "She told you that you were at the edge of your biggest adventure. What is it?"

I keep a tight grip on her hand and make her follow me over more slippery rocks, deciding not to answer. To speak about it would mean I actually believed in Bre'Shun's assumption...which I don't. She's a fairy, but even they can be wrong sometimes.

Or so I pray.

A queasy feeling takes over my stomach. Their track record of being right is one-hundred percent. I'm doomed.

"You have to be careful with those gaps," I mumble over my shoulder, taking care that I climb at a pace right for Angel's shorter legs.

"Since you obviously aren't going to answer my question, can I ask you something else?" her disappointed words drift to me.

"Maybe."

"What is in that little chest with the treasure?"

This is a question I can answer without feeling sick. "A watch."

"Seriously?" Angel pulls me to a stop, making me face her disbelieving eyes. "What's so special about a watch that you carry the key to it around your neck all the time?"

Automatically, I reach to my collar and feel the key under my shirt, frowning at her. "How do you— Ah, Peter Pan." The scamp certainly told her. I place my hands on her hips and lift her from her rock down to mine. She steadies herself with her hands on my shoulders. When she stands, she slides them down to my chest until she finds the key. I lay my hand over hers to keep it in place. "It's the key to *tomorrow*."

Her forehead creases at her thoughts. "Bre'Shun mentioned that, too. I don't get it."

Smoothing the deep V between her brows with my thumbs, I explain, "A long time ago, something terrible happened in Peter Pan's life. It devastated him and he decided to never grow up." I remember how I felt when the same terrible thing happened to me long before and how it tore a piece of my heart out. Sometimes I can't even be mad at Peter for his actions. "With his furious decision he sort of hexed Neverland. And every hex needs to be tied to an object. Or so I've been told by the fairies anyway. It's a symbol for the spell."

Angel's brown eyes grow bigger with understanding. "So for stopping time, the charm was tied to a watch."

"By the fairies, yes. They gave it to me in a chest with the key. But it's not just any watch. It was my father's. *Our* father's." I let go of her and continue to descend the rocky tongue of land. The half moon reflects in the water beside us. Without its light, it would be too dark to even see my hand in front of my face now.

"You know," I hear Angel from behind, "ever since we met Peter in the jungle, I was wondering how you could be brothers and still hate each other so."

"We're only half brothers. That's why." This is really a part of my life that I don't like talking about, but if I want Angel to understand, there's no other choice. "My mother was twenty when she met my father. She fell in love with him in an instant. He was a charming man." I realize the irony of what I'm going to say next and grin at Angel over my shoulder. "He was a pirate."

She smiles back.

"Within the year, she had me. As I grew up, I didn't see my father very often, but I do remember how proud he was when he brought me to his ship for the first time. I was around five then." I think I hear something in the water, so I stop and listen, but the sea is calm. There's no mermaid around yet. I sigh and walk on. "My mother died when I was twelve."

Angel's fingers tighten around my hand. "I'm sorry, Jamie."

I nod in the dark, accepting her compassion. "My father never came back for me after that and it didn't take me long to find out why. Shortly after he met my mother, he fell in love with another woman. They had a son, too."

"Peter," Angel gasps. "It must have been hard to find out when you were already grieving over your mother's death."

It was like a slap in my face. I had never felt that broken before. And never again afterward. Clenching my jaw, I let go of Angel's hand. "I didn't care."

We reach the pointy land's end. Here's a good place to sit and wait for the fish girls to show up. I step to the last rock then help Angel down. She studies my face as if searching for the truth I try to hide. To escape her gaze, I lower to the smooth rock that still bears the warmth of the day, but she squats in front of me and places her hands on my bent knees. "How much older than Peter are you?"

This could be fun, I realize with a notch of sarcasm. "How old do you think I am, Angel?"

"I don't know. Around twenty-three or a little younger."

I laugh. The sound scares me, because it's filled with pain. "I'd just turned nineteen when Peter decided to stay a child forever and therewith changed the fate of everyone living in Neverland."

At my words, Angel tips to her side and lands on her behind. Yeah, she didn't expect me to be so young. But then I've been nineteen for so long, I lost count of the years.

"Do you know why Peter made that decision?"

Sadly, I do. "After I found out the truth, I gave Peter hell. I hated him with a passion for stealing my father."

"But it wasn't his fault."

So what? It wasn't my fault either, goddammit. "I was a kid. All I knew was that my mother had died and my father chose a different son over me."

"I see." Scooting closer, Angel leans her head against my shoulder and takes my hand, intertwining our fingers. "Did Peter know you two were half brothers?"

I stare at our joined hands for a long moment. "Not at first. One day down by the shore, I had him on the ground with my knee on his chest. He begged me to let him go. I didn't. Then he cried at my face why I was doing these things to him?"

"Did you tell him?"

I shake my head. "Not that day."

Her head tilts up and I feel her gaze on my face. "When did he find out?"

"I told him a couple years later, after I had sliced his arm with a dagger from the elbow to his shoulder." Pausing at this particular memory, I feel my throat tighten. The day ended with a tragedy. "Peter was stunned by the revelation. For the first time since I had lost my mother—and my father—I felt a small bit of victory over Peter."

"What happened then?"

Cold comes over me. I know it's not from the night, but from the pictures surfacing in my mind. Longing for a little comfort, I move my arm behind Angel and pull her in front of me to have her sitting between my legs like last night. She curls up against my chest and skims her fingers over my heart in caressing circles. I stroke her back up and down. "When he came around," I tell her in a lower voice than before, "he ran home and asked his mother about it. She had no idea."

"It destroyed their family?"

"Worse. When Peter's mother found out about me—about her husband lying to her all those years—it was too much for her to cope. She ran to a cliff and jumped, trying to end her life."

Angel stiffens in my arms. I wrap them tighter around her. No matter what she thinks of me right now, I don't want her to move away from me. She's warm. She's my comfort. "Our father was close behind her, but he couldn't reach her in time. He wanted to save her and jumped, too. None of them came out of the water again." I pause and dip my head to smell her soft hair. "Peter and I were there. We saw it happen."

A melancholic silence lasts for minutes between us. Then Angel takes my hand and places a kiss on my knuckles. "I can only imagine how it would kill me if I ever lost *my* family. My sisters. It must have been so hard for you two to deal with this."

I've never looked at Angel's situation from her side, what she's going to lose when she can't go home. I drag in a long breath and tell her, "It was hard for me. But it was *impossible* for Peter. You see, for one, there was me, who'd tortured him all through his childhood. Then there was our father who built this bubble of lies. And in the end there was his own mother who didn't even think about him when she made that fatal decision to jump. It destroyed him. He needed a way to escape. And he found it with the hex. Forever a child, he thought, he didn't have to deal with his loss. Children play. They forget. So did Peter. And the Pan was born."

"Poor Peter. It must take a lot for a child to make a desperate decision like he did. And I'm sorry about your family, too, Jamie."

"Don't be. It all happened a very long time ago. I don't think about it often." The mood has gone downward for long enough. I don't want her to feel sorry for me, and I don't want to dwell on my past anymore, so I force a smile and add, "Unless, once in a while, a strange young woman comes from a different world and turns my life upside down."

Angel catches on my change of mood and grins. "Yeah, I've heard such things happen from time to time. Especially when these women need rescuing from a deadly trap in the jungle."

Her words carry me back to that night. Particularly to the moment when Peter turned his back on her. He was so hurt. And I'd just now figured out why. "Did you know that you look a lot like Peter's mother? You have the same dark hair and big brown eyes. I think you remind him of her."

Angel hums a *hm*. "It might be the reason why he was so angry when I said I wanted to go back to my world."

"And then he saw you with me and he thought you'd betrayed him, like his mother did when she left him alone."

"Yes. It makes sense. He still misses her. And I guess you're missing your family, too." She picks a stone from the gap between the rocks next to her and tosses it into the waves. "So now you want that chest with your father's watch back for...a memento?"

I reach for a handful of pebbles too and toss them, telling her, "I want to find it so I can destroy it."

"Why would you do that?"

"It's hard to explain."

"Try."

All right. I settle back against the big rock behind me and gaze at the stars. "When Peter decided to never grow up, it was such a grave wish that it affected all of Neverland. No one has aged a day ever since then. Life on this isle continues, just not the way you would expect it. Even though people do different things every day, they aren't getting on with their lives. It's an endless loop and nobody notices."

"Nobody? Why do you know about it then?"

"I was wondering that myself." For years and years. It's still weird to go to the port and see the same woman pregnant for decades, or the children never growing older. No one gets born, no one dies. It's all the same, every new damn day. "My only answer is that it must be linked to us being brothers. Or maybe because I was the one who started it by destroying his family. Who knows?" I let go of a long sigh. Not even the fairies would tell me why I'm the only one who feels odd when everyone else is happy every new morning.

"When I first met Peter and the Lost Boys, they told me about you," Angel says softly.

I grin and brush the tip of her nose with my finger. "Mean and ugly, I know."

That makes her laugh. "Yes. But it's different. I mean different from what you told me. Peter thinks this is all just a game. He doesn't take you seriously."

"Mm." I nod. "That's what I meant before. Children forget. Our fights have become a game for him. Stealing my treasure was his greatest coup. Unfortunately, he stole the chest with it."

"Why did you keep the watch in a chest anyway? If you wanted to destroy it and undo the spell, you should have done so the first chance you got."

"That wasn't possible. I can't destroy the charm. Only Peter can because he initiated it. I was trying to find a way to make him do it." I shrug. "As you see, I failed."

"He thinks something very dear to you is inside that chest."

I waggle my brows deviously at her. "He's right."

Angel sits up on her knees and looks me sternly in the eyes. She pouts sweetly then her brows knit together in the mockery of accusation. I don't know if I should take her serious now or if she's going to laugh at me. Then she smacks me playfully on the shoulder. "So you didn't really want to help me find my home to make up for being so cruel in the jungle, you rascal! All the time, you only wanted the location of the chest's hiding place."

I lean forward with a smirk and slip my hand to the back of her neck. "Of course." Then I yank her closer and kiss her delectable lips.

Nothing ever tasted as good as Angel. I nibble and kiss her bottom lip until she starts to smile against my mouth and kisses me back. Her shyness of last night entirely gone, she lets me pull her into me, sits between my legs again and digs her fingers into my shirt.

I feel a longing for this girl I can barely control. Finding her hands, I lace my fingers with hers from the back and move them up to my open collar. I want to feel her skin on mine, if only this little part of it. Her hands are cotton-soft, her fingers exploring. They crawl up behind my neck and run through my hair. Shudders of pleasure race through me. I do the same to her, letting her silky hair flow through my splayed fingers. Angel is amazing. She *feels* amazing. I never want to let her go.

Tracing my tongue first over her bottom lip then over her top lip, I explore every little bow and valley of them. They are perfect to kiss. I skim her hair aside and hook it behind her ear. There's a spot right behind that I know makes her shiver when I kiss it. It's been tempting me all day. Seductively slow, I run my tongue all the way around the shell of her ear. Angel giggles and the expected shiver travels through her body. It's exhilarating. I take her earlobe between my teeth and nibble. Delicious.

"You're a ruthless man, James Hook," she whispers as I trail a path of kisses down the column of her throat.

It makes me chuckle against her downy skin. "Yes, I am." And she hasn't even seen half of it yet. But she's also the only person in my world who gets to see *this* side of me. The side that tempts me to lose myself. My pirate side starts to crumble in front of her. And I'm in no hurry to pick up the pieces.

I lean back, dragging her with me. Our kiss turns deep and salacious, our tongues sliding against each other in slow, demanding moves. I want to eat her up, drink her in and breathe all of her. However many more days I have with her, they can never be enough. Angel fits against me like she's my long-missed other part. Everything is perfect about her. She completes me. I hold her tighter, afraid this is only a dream and she'll be gone when I open my eyes.

But when I blink, she's still here. And she smiles at me. "You look surprised."

I press a soft kiss to her brow. "Not surprised. Just happy." For once. After a very long time.

Angel giggles again. I love that sound. "Has that anything to do with me?" she teases.

"It has all to do with you," I confess and stroke her soft hair out of her face.

Her warm smile returns. "I like that." Covered with my cape, she nestles against me. I hold her tight and start to draw small circles at the back of her neck with my fingers. After some time, I just shape my palm to the side of her face and skim my thumb back and forth over her cheekbone. Her body twitches a couple of times as she drifts off to sleep in my arms. I don't stop caressing her.

Hours tick away. Slowly the moon wanders from my left to my right. In the distance the stars blink like they're smirking down at me. I bend one knee and rest my arm on it. The night sky has never been more beautiful.

A heavy tiredness creeps over me. To keep a tight watch on the sea for any sign of the mermaids, I can't allow myself to follow Angel to the land of dreams. I ignore the pull of sleep and in my mind relive the time I've had with her instead. It's been only three days, but when I press a kiss to the top of her head and rest my cheek against it, feeling her content sigh against my chest, it seems like we've know each other far longer than that.

The sea is calmest shortly before dawn, so I realize I've been sitting with Angel for the entire night. And though my bones are stiff and cold and my back hurts, I enjoyed every minute of it.

"Thanks for trying to help me, Jamie," she mumbles.

Hearing her voice again after the silent hours brings a smile to my face. "You're welcome." I caress her hair. "Did you sleep well?"

"No, it's never been there."

"What?" I frown and look down at her face. Her eyes are still closed. "Angel?"

"It's the wrong place," she whispers. "Not in the jungle."

"Angel? Are you awake?"

"A place you can't reach...in the water...not on the island."

"What is not—" *Sink me!* She's talking about the treasure. And she's still asleep. My heart pounds harder.

I'm afraid it might wake her. When she doesn't say more for a couple of minutes, I lean down to her ear and say softly, "Where is it, Angel?"

She sighs. Her warm breath feathers against my skin at my open collar. "In a cave...the rocks that look like a birthday cake...out here...can find it at low tide..."

Rocks offshore? North of Neverland? Low tide is a problem with the Jolly Roger. That part of the sea is rockier than at any other side. We can't sail there. But if we take a dinghy—

Something splashes in the water fifty feet ahead. The mermaids. They have finally come.

If they'd shown up only ten minutes sooner, I would have called to them in an instant. I would have woken Angel and tried to reason with the fish girls to deliver our message to Peter. Now...I wonder what will happen if I don't.

I have all the answers. Without her knowing, Angel told me where the treasure is. It's only a matter of time now until my men find the rocks that look like a birthday cake at low tide.

One of the mermaids breaks away from her folks and warily swims closer. Her dark hair floats in the water. She locks her eyes with mine. Of course she knows who I am. And still, something draws her in. Her shoulders emerge from the water as she quietly bobs up and down with the gentle waves. She's curious, I can tell. When her gaze skates to the girl in my arms, recognition flickers in her eyes. They must have met before. She looks at me again, tilting her head. I manage an odd smile.

If I don't talk to her now, she might just dip underwater and be gone the next minute. There would be no other way to find Peter Pan.

A selfish thought invades my mind. I don't have to take Angel home. She already told me where to find the treasure and the chest. I could keep her. Forever in Neverland. With me. Ignoring the fish girl in the water next to us, I cradle Angel's head in my hands and, closing my eyes, I run my lips across her downy brow. I *want* to keep her. More than I want that damn treasure or the watch.

With a hurtful clarity, I realize the fairy was right after all. I'm at the edge of my biggest adventure. And I want to be selfish.

Chapter 11

Soft mumbling wakes me from a sweet dream about Jamie. I thought I heard his voice, but it could have been me speaking in my sleep that brought me back to Neverland's reality at dawn.

Jamie's lips are pressed to my forehead and he holds my hair tight at the back of my head. I look up and meet his warm eyes, but beneath them looms a layer of divisiveness. Maybe I can chase it away with a smile. "Hi."

"Good morning," he replies softly. "Did you sleep well on me?"

"Perfectly well," I assure him. "You look tired, though. You didn't sleep much, did you?"

"I didn't sleep at all. Someone had to watch over you." He graces my cheekbone with his knuckle.

Behind me something splashes in the water. I jerk around and glimpse a shimmering blue fishtail disappearing in the waves. Turning around, I beam at Jamie. "Was that a mermaid?" He nods but he doesn't look as euphoric as I am. I know that we came here last night to see one, but for some weird reason I can't recall why. "I heard you saying something. Did you talk to her?"

Jamie stares at me for an uncomfortably long time before he nods once. What the heck is up with him? I pout playfully and rub the frown away from his brow. "What did you two talk about?"

More silence follows. Jamie cocks his head, eyeing me warily. Then he says with a slight edge to his voice, "I told her I want to offer Peter a truce."

"Right..." I mumble, suddenly confused, and scratch my eyebrow, lowering my gaze to the rocks beneath me. Something about all this should ring a bell. But it just doesn't. "And why did you do that?"

Jamie cups my chin and tilts my face so I stare straight into his eyes again. "Angel, what exactly do you remember?"

"Huh?" What stupid question is that, for Christ's sake? "Why, everything. You brought me out here last night." A titillating grin slips to my lips. "And you kissed me."

His features become graver than I ever remember seeing. "Before that," he clarifies.

"Before that we were on your ship. And you kissed me there, too." I can't seem to stop smiling this morning.

"That is not what I meant," he almost growls at me now. Then he rubs his hands over his face. When they drop to my shoulders, he looks me sternly in the eye. "What happened in your life last week? Or the last month? Where do you come from, Angel?" He speaks with such a low voice that a shiver races along my skin.

"I guess I've been somewhere, doing stuff." The word *London* ghosts around in my mind. Maybe that is the answer. But all I connect with it are two young faces in the shadows. I don't know who these girls are. And I actually don't care. I want to dig out the cheerful Jamie again, so I nudge his nose with the tip of mine. "Why do you want to know?"

He hesitates. "You seem different this morning."

Do I? "Well, after spending the night with you I'm just happy. Is that okay with you, Captain Hook?" I tease him and place a quick kiss on his cheek.

He opens his mouth to say something, but nothing comes out and after a second he closes it again. The left side of his lips twitches slowly into a smirk. "I guess it is." He rises to his feet and pulls me up with him, taking my hand and looking much happier than before. "Come on, let's go. We're done here."

Jamie helps me climb the way back over the rocks, never missing a chance to hold me for a moment after lifting me over each gap. Just before we reach land again, I sling my arms around his neck and kiss him. "What's your plan for today?"

"I don't know. You tell me." His eyes are shining now.

With my forefinger pressed to my lips, I cock my head, watching two seagulls sail in the breeze. "Hm, what's a good way to spend a day in Neverland? Oh, I know." I waggle my brows. "We could cruise around the island. And you could let me steer the ship."

Jamie laughs my favorite warm sound. "You're easy to please today."

"Aren't I always?"

"Not quite so much."

Whatever that means... I shrug and lace my fingers with his, swinging our hands between us as we wander along the path close to the shore. After a while, Jamie wraps his arm around my shoulders without letting go of my hand. "Do you remember where we went yesterday?" he asks.

"Sure. We went into the forest and you introduced me to the fairies."

"For what reason?"

I shrug. "For fun?"

He eyes me sideways, his mood taking a turn to serious again. "When we sailed out with the Jolly Roger two days ago, where were we headed?"

"Around the island."

"For what purpose?"

I stop and turn to face him, placing both my hands on his stomach. "Jamie, your questions are starting to freak me out. What is it?"

He stares at me for so long I feel the hair at the back of my neck bristle. But then he shrugs and shakes his head, the creases in his brows easing. "Nothing. Forget what I said."

Forget what I said... Forget. The word rings with misgivings in my ears. All of a sudden, I feel awkward and place a hand to my stomach. My gaze sinks to the ground. Should I be somewhere else right now? I know that Neverland hasn't been my home for long, but now I'm here and I like it. There's no reason to think about what I did last week or last month. Now is what counts. And I'm happy now.

Jamie grabs my shoulders and angles his head to look at my face. "Are you all right?"

"Yes." I give him a cheeky smile. "I'm just hungry as hell."

"Let's get back to the ship and feed you then." With his arm around my waist underneath his cape that I'm still wearing, he pulls me into his side and we stroll on.

After some time of gazing out on the sea, my mind wanders to the busy seaport and off to the fairies close by. "Hey," I say to Jamie. "Wouldn't it be fantastic to live in a house in the forest, just like Bre'Shun and Remona?"

"You liked it there?"

Leaning my head against his shoulder, I sigh. "It was beautiful."

"We can build you one." He chuckles and places a kiss on top of my head as we walk. "And then I'll come to visit you every day, and you can cook me dinner."

"Or I'll come to visit you on the ship," I counter, skipping ahead and turning. With my hands braced on his chest, I walk a few steps backward and smirk up at him. "And you can teach me how to be a cool captain. You can let me wear your hat again."

He takes my hand and tucks me under his arm at his other side. "It'll freak Smee out for sure." The thought makes us both laugh. "We would have to find an awesome pirate name for you."

"So? What were you thinking?"

Jamie shrugs. "It's not something you just make up. The name must describe you somehow. Let me watch you for a little longer and I'll come up with something nice."

I huddle happily against Jamie, drawing in a deep breath of his enticing scent. The warm morning sun smiles at my face and the mellow songs of birds drift to us from all sides. Waves rolling leisurely to the shore complete this perfect picture. I wouldn't want to be anywhere else at this moment. In fact, I don't want to be anywhere else than in Jamie's arms ever again. He's the man I've been waiting for. Gorgeous, caring, and with the right bit of danger underneath. He's perfect. And I'm on the brink of falling in love with him.

Not long after, we reach the boat that Jamie tied to a rock by the shore. Giving me a hand when I climb in, he follows after me and sits with his back to the bow. His pecs, biceps and abs twitch every time he rows. I could watch him doing this all day.

As we near the Jolly Roger, the guy that usually hangs out on top of the highest mast bends out of his basket and shouts to the crew, "Cap'n's back!" Immediately, Brant Skyler with his red bandana and shaggy-haired Smee come to help us moor the boat.

When all the men on deck see that I'm wearing Jamie's cape and how he holds my hand even after I've climbed over the railing, lewd chatter starts and they throw juicy looks my way. Some of them even catcall.

I find this amusing. Jamie, not so much. He lets go of my hand and barks at the men, "Shut up, ye bilge rats and get to work! Take her a mile out and then head north!"

The crew hurries around on deck, nearly tripping over each other's feet. They pull some ropes and the next second the Jolly Roger's mighty white sails drop and billow in the wind. Craning my neck, I stare with an open mouth.

"You know, if you don't want to live in that house in the forest all by yourself, I'll always have a cabin for you on this ship," Jamie says into my ear from behind.

I turn my head to him. "Nice offer, Captain. I might

just consider it."

"I hope so." He massages the spot between my shoulder blades. "How do you feel?"

Looking down at myself, I grimace and tell him, "A little mucky. But fantastic otherwise."

"The crew normally takes a jump into the water for a quick wash, but I figure that's not quite your style." He smiles. "You can use the shower in my quarters, if you want. I was going to take one myself and I'll have Skyler refill the buckets for you later."

I nod and follow him with my eyes as he leaves for his cabin. It's much too warm for wearing his cape now, so I take it off, spread it on the boxes that we'd been sitting on the other night and settle in to watch the men moving about on the ship. It's all so interesting and new. Wondering where I would fit into the crew, my gaze lands on the guy at the top of the mast. He's holding a spyglass and scans the surroundings. With my small girl-hands, I'm certainly not made for hoisting the sails or dropping anchor, but keeping watch is something I can see myself doing. I'd be a real member of Jamie's crew then. A *pirate*. I giggle and shudder with excitement.

The island is shrinking behind us as we cruise out on the gentle waves. After half an hour, it's time to take up Jamie's offer and wash myself. Skyler carried two buckets of water through his door a few minutes ago, so Jamie is probably done by now.

Tucking the cape under my arm, I walk to his quarters and knock on the door. When he opens, my mouth instantly starts to water. So many muscles under so much naked skin. My fingers itch to skim over his chest.

Buckling his belt, Jamie steps away from the doorway. "Coming for the shower?" He pulls a fresh white shirt over his shoulders and pushes his arms through the sleeves.

For that and the nice view. I nod and suppress a grin.

"Make yourself at home then. I'll be in my study until you're done." The door next to the small table in his cabin is still wide open and askew—only attached to one broken hinge. He walks away, and I hurry to the bathroom. The floor is wet from his shower. Careful not to slip, I pull off my dress and hang it on a hook on the door for later. The water is even colder this time, but the tangerine-scented soap still smells as good as ever.

Clean, dressed, and feeling fabulous, I enter Jamie's bedroom, running my fingers through my hair a few times to detangle the knots. The place is empty, so I peek around the corner into his study. He's sitting in his chair behind the desk. Arms folded on the wooden surface, he's slumped forward, his cheek resting in the crook of his elbow. Beside him lies the big black pirate hat with the fluffy feather. Poor guy—he told me he was awake all night. Now it seems sleep has caught up with him.

On tiptoes I walk closer and study his relaxed face.

His wet hair falls seductively over his forehead, entangling with his long lashes. In the silent room, his deep, even breaths are the only sound. A smile forms on my lips as I squat beside him.

Tenderly, I brush my fingertips through his hair, run them behind his ear, down his neck and along his arm to the back of his hand. It's bigger than mine. Although he's the captain of this ship, he's not the one doing work, I realize. Or maybe it's *because* he's the captain. His hands are slightly callused but clean, his nails cut short. His fingers look strong, but I know how gentle they can be...when he touches me.

When my gaze wanders back to his face, I suck in a breath. His eyes are open. Striking blue and curious, they are focused on mine. Jamie doesn't move or say a word. Only his wet strands of hair twitch every time he blinks. In this short unreal moment, he truly looks nineteen.

My hand is still splayed over his. I pull it away and start to stand up, but he laces his fingers with mine and holds me in place. Trapped in his gaze, I can't look away.

Not sure what to do and because I don't want to break this special moment of ours alone, I fold my arms on the desk like he's doing and lay my head on them. We're face to face, with only five inches between us, and our fingers locked. All I see is his warm blue eyes. His scent surrounds me. I feel him deeper in my heart, like I'm just beginning to know him.

There's so much more beneath this pirate's ruthlessness. A part he hasn't opened to anyone other than me. And I'm starting to crave this part of him with everything I have.

Never breaking eye contact, Jamie slips out his other arm from under his cheek, slowly reaches for the hat beside him, and places it on my head. It's sitting askew and covers my right eye. I feel roguish. The shadow of a smile sneaks to his lips.

"Hey," I whisper.

"Hi," he says back.

"You fell asleep."

"It was a long night."

"Do you want me to leave so you can rest?"

He skims a few stray wisps of my hair out of my forehead and under the hat, hooking them behind my ear. His warm hand splays over my neck and his thumb starts stroking along my jaw. He shakes his head. And I smile.

"Shall we go outside?" I suggest then. "It's such a lovely day."

Dragging a deep sigh, Jamie straightens in his chair and rubs his hands over his face. "You go ahead. I'll be with you in a minute."

He does look tired and somehow worn out. Deciding to give him time, I stand and face him. I must look like a princess playing pirate in my current outfit, so I give him the hat back and tuck my hands into the pockets of my dress, rocking on the balls of my feet. "Can you show me how to work the helm again?"

"We can do whatever you like." He reaches for my wrist and pulls my hand out of my pocket. A small piece of paper slips out with it and spirals to the floor.

I bend to pick it up, briefly glance at it, then scrunch it between my fingers and toss it into the basket next to the desk. As I turn to leave, Jamie grabs a handful of my dress and holds me back. "What did you throw away?"

I shrug. "Nothing important. Just a forgotten price tag or something."

His brows furrow. He leans over and fishes the paper out of the bin. With his thumbs, he smoothes it out and stares at it for a long moment, then his gaze lifts to mine. "This isn't a price tag, Angel." He pauses then speaks with more insistence. "It's a ticket for transport."

"Okay..." I arch both my eyebrows at him. "But I don't intend to go anywhere."

"It's a ticket to *London*. Where you come from."

"So?"

"So...you shouldn't throw this away."

I shrug. If it means so much to him, he can keep it. I don't mind. "See you outside," I say and, in a happy stride, I walk on deck.

Finding a place to stand by the railing, I prop my elbows on it and gaze down into the water. It's crystal clear. Under the surface the pretty coral reefs shine and colorful fish zoom past. Neverland is so beautiful. Everything about it. It doesn't matter where I came from; I never want to leave again.

Expecting Jamie to follow me out here, I cast a glance over my shoulder. The door to his study is still open. I can see him pace his room. When he stops moving in circles, he lifts his gaze to the ceiling and rakes his hands through his hair. Something is nagging at him. Is this still about the price tag? I can even see his chest lifting with a heavy sigh. Then he braces his hands on the desk and hangs his head.

Even though I'm clueless, my heart fills with sadness for him. I push away from the railing and hasten across the quarter deck toward his study. But before I make it there, he steps out and stops when he sees me. His face is marred with longing and determination. He's still clasping the price tag in his right hand. A bad feeling creeps to my stomach.

"What's wrong?" I whisper.

"We need to talk."

These four words make my blood run cold.

"There's something you have to know," he tells me in a tight voice. "And it'll change everything."

My heart misses a beat. I don't want things to change. It's good how it is. I take a step back, shaking my head. My knees start to tremble. Suddenly I don't want to know what's going on anymore. I don't want to talk. Not when the subject is causing him so much pain that it shows in every line of his face. And I realize it's all about me.

"We can talk about it another time," I croak. "Tomorrow..."

Jamie follows as I stumble backward. He grabs my shoulders and pulls me to a halt. "No, we cannot talk about it tomorrow. It'll be too late then." He drags a restless hand through his hair and cuts a glance skyward. "Shit, it might already be too late now!"

Every pirate on board stops work for a moment and turns to us. Jamie doesn't even notice. I do. "You can't stay in Neverland," he says through clenched teeth.

My world quakes. "What?"

"You have to go home."

"I don't understand." What I really want to say is *I don't want to hear this*. Has he already had enough of me?

"This isn't the right place for you," Jamie explains. "Hell, I wish it was, but it just isn't. You belong somewhere else."

"Someplace where *you aren't*? Is that what you're trying to tell me?" I cock my head. "You no longer want me near you?"

Honest shock narrows his eyes. "No! God, *no*!" He takes my face between his hands and touches his brow to mine, pressing his lips together and squeezing his eyes shut. "I would tie you to me and never let you go, if I could, Angel."

"Then what is this all about?" My voice breaks on the last three words.

Jamie swallows hard. "This"—he holds out the price tag—"is a *train...ticket...*to *London.*" He sounds like he's recalling the words from somewhere at the back of his mind. "The city where you were born. Where you *live.* You've been trying to get back ever since we met, but you kept forgetting things about your past." His face scrunches up. "And I ignored it."

Deep inside me, something rings true about his words, but it's so far away that I can't reach it. And I don't even want to try. "What's it to you where I come from?"

"It means something to me, because I care for you, Angel. I promised to help you find home. Just try to remember! It's there *somewhere.*" He skims my hair out of my forehead and hooks it behind my ears, resting his hands on my neck.

Suddenly I hear the voices of two girls calling my name. They step out of the shadows in my mind. One is a pixie. The other holds out a picture book. I know these girls. They are... "Family," I whisper hoarsely.

My heart sinks to the floorboards of the Jolly Roger. With trembling knees I walk backward until I feel the wooden boxes pushing against my legs and slump down. "But I don't want to go," I breathe as Jamie lowers to a crouch in front of me.

"And I don't want you to leave. All night I was thinking of ways to keep you. You're the best thing I've ever had. But I realize now it's selfish to force you to stay."

He wouldn't have to force me. I *want* to be with him. I want to feel his warmth as his arms wrap around me. "Be selfish then. I don't care."

"Heck, Angel, I tried!" He sighs. "But I can't be selfish with you…"

"Why not? You're a pirate. You've been selfish most of your life," I snap.

"Yes. About things that never really mattered to me. With you it's different." He drops forward to his knees, the hard lines of his face growing softer. "I want you to be happy…more than I want you to myself."

"And you think I would be happy if you sent me back to…wherever it is that I come from?"

"Back to London. Yes. It's a world full of wonder. You have ships on wheels there that go with an amazing speed. Your horses might as well have wings, because you fly in coaches." His eyes grow wide with newfound enthusiasm. "Boxes write letters for you and you can talk to people across the world through tiny things you call a *John.*"

Vaguely I recall holding one of these devices to my ear and talking to somebody, but I'm sure I didn't call it *John.* Grimacing, I struggle to remember more of these things he's talking about. I can hear some honking in my mind. And the chimes of a clock.

Jamie reaches for my hand and twists my wrist. "Look at this."

I look down at the tattoo on my forearm. It's almost gone. Only the first letter and a few stars of the dusting beneath are still visible.

"Your baby sister gave it to you." He searches my face. "She's your everything. Both your sisters are. After they were born you carried them around all day as if you were their mother. At night you sneaked into their room with your bed linen and slept on the floor beside their beds. You call them honey bunny and fairy bug—even though I think that one's more of a pixie."

Paulina and Brittney Renae. "How do you—"

"How do I know? Think, Angel! You told me all about your life the other night and made me promise to retell it. You knew you'd forget your world. Neverland is doing this to you. It wants you to forget." He shapes his palms to my cheeks and touches his forehead to mine. "I'm keeping my promise. Now don't make this any harder for me than it already is."

Yes, he kept his promise. All our conversations of the past few days suddenly resurface with crystal clarity. Everything he told me about Peter Pan and their father. Everything I told him about my home, my house and my family. My heart swells with longing for my sisters. I know where I come from. I remember why I need to go back.

But most of all, I remember what Jamie gets out of this deal if he can take me home.

My voice drops to an ice-cold level. "You're only doing this because you want me to tell you where the treasure is."

James Hook

What the hell— I suck in a sharp breath. "Angel, are you crazy?"

"I haven't been this clear in my mind since I came to Neverland." She rises from the box and looks down at me with venom in her gaze. "You promised to bring me home. And in turn you want me to tell you where to find that freaking treasure of yours."

My shoulders slump. "Yes, I did. But it's not why I'm trying to help you now."

"No? Then why, *Captain*? Because you've suddenly grown a heart?" She laughs. The sound is bitter. "I don't think so."

"Angel—"

"You know what? I think you're afraid that with me forgetting things you'll never find what you want. And then I'm of no use to you any longer."

I can hardly believe she means what she's saying. After what we had the past few days. What we had become. Pushing to my feet, I grab her shoulders and shake her once, making her look at my face. "This is *bullshit*. And you know it!"

"Until ten minutes ago I only knew that I really liked being with you. And you're going to throw it all away. Because you're selfish!"

Goddammit, for once in my life I'm *not* selfish and here's what I get for it. But I won't let this silly lass get away with playing down my feelings for her. Wrapping my fingers around her wrist, I haul her down the stairs to the main deck, across, and up to the fore deck. We've just passed Mermaid Lagoon and are still heading north. Pushing her against the railing of the ship's bow with my body, I snarl into her ear, "Where do you think we're sailing, Angel? What's out there?"

The tension in her body reveals how angry she really is at me, but she's silent for a moment and just stares ahead.

"You know what's hidden here. What we can only find at low tide." I struggle to kick the edge out of my voice again as I spin her around to face me. "There's a treasure buried underwater, isn't there?"

Her mouth and eyes open wide. She takes a few steadying breaths, her hands finding balance on my forearms. "You already know?"

"Heck, yes, I do. Wanna know how I found out?" I take her silence for a yes. "You were talking in your sleep again out on the rocks where you freakin' slept on my chest and in my arms. With me taking care of you all night."

Angel gasps. "But why didn't you tell me?" The rush of the waves swallows her whisper.

"I told you: because I wanted to be selfish. You were all different this morning. You had forgotten. And I wanted to keep you with me. But dammit, Angel, I can't be selfish with you!" I grit my teeth. "I just can't."

She doesn't say a word for an unbearably long time. *Come on,* I want to shout at her. *You must see that I'm telling the truth!*

Eventually, her hands slip away from my arms. She swallows hard and tears start to glisten in her eyes. "If I go home, I'll never see you again."

My throat tightens. "I know." And the thought kills me. I hug her and rest my chin on the top of her head. "But you'll be reunited with your sisters. You'll be happy again. And one day you'll just forget me and continue to live your life in London like you did before." I didn't mean for this to sound so sad. However, my attempt at soothing her backfires. Her hot tears seep into my shirt.

This time, I'm not telling her to stop crying. I just hold her for a long time, caress her hair, and fight to get rid of the bile in my throat. If all the right decisions hurt this much, I swear I'll not make another in my life.

"Cap'n!" Brant Skyler's surprised call drifts to us.

"It's Pan!"

Not releasing Angel just yet, I look over my shoulder. Peter Pan has come indeed. He's sitting on the crosspiece of the ship's front mast, feet dangling, a stupid grin pasted on his face as always. He's arguing with Smee about whether he's going to piss down on his head or not.

Skyler pulls a pistol from his belt and aims at Peter. "Put it away, Yarrin' Brant," I shout out to him. Then I press a soft kiss behind Angel's ear. "Your ticket home has arrived."

She sighs and dabs at her cheeks when I release her. "How will we get him to teach me?"

"Leave that to me." I take her hand and walk to Peter's mast. Right underneath, I tilt my head and shout, "Pan, you filthy little bastard! Get your ass down here!"

"Very subtle," Angel grunts behind me.

"What? It's the best way to catch his attention." And it sure as hell works.

Peter stops midsentence and moves his gaze to me. "Is this your idea of a truce? Your pet pirate threatening to cut my fingers and toes one by one and your watchdog trying to shoot me?"

"A truce?" half of my crew blurt at once.

"Get a grip, men," I snarl at them. "This is just temporary." Then I call out to Peter, "No one's going to touch you. Come down and we talk."

"Ah, I don't think so. I'm actually enjoying the view

up here," he counters. "Tell me what you want, Smellin' Jim Hook, and it better be something good, or I'll be off with the next breeze."

Same old, same old. I'm tempted to pull Brant Skyler's pistol and shoot the kid myself. For Angel's sake I clamp down on my temper. "I— *We* need your help to send Angel back to her world."

"Back to her world? What's wrong with yours? Last time I saw her, she was quite happy to be a pirate."

"Last time you saw her, she was hanging over sharpened pikes and you just walked away, you nasty piece of shit!"

Peter clicks his tongue then he laughs dryly. "Why are you wasting my time, Hook?"

Angel squeezes my hand. Turning, I face her disapproving scowl. All right. I'll try this differently then. "Listen," I shout to Peter and pinch the bridge of my nose. "I know you think Angel betrayed you. But you're wrong. I kidnapped her, took her to my ship and made her walk with me through the jungle to show me your den. She didn't reveal where you lived nor where the treasure is hidden even though I threatened her with death." I pause and clear my throat. Now comes the tricky part. "Angel needs to learn to fly to get home. You're the only frea—" I cut myself off and quickly correct to, "The only *guy* I know who is able to fly without wings. I want you to teach her." And then I add through gritted teeth, *"Please."*

Stunned, Peter hesitates a long moment. But something must have impressed him, because he slides down from the crosspiece then and lowers to the deck. Wary as always, he takes care to keep out of anybody's reach and leaps on the railing.

His focus is only on Angel. "Why do you want to go back?" he asks her with a friendlier voice than when he was talking to me.

Angel steps around me, but she doesn't release my hand. "Because I have a family, Peter. A mother and a father who are waiting for me. And two little sisters. It would break their hearts if I didn't come back."

It's a smart thing to play the family card with Peter. It'll remind him of how much he missed his mother when she left him behind. But for Angel it's the truth after all. There are people waiting for her. People who care for her. They must be worried like hell.

Peter cocks his head. "And why do you need to fly to go back?"

"A fairy said I can only leave Neverland the way I came here."

Nodding, he levitates a few feet up, crosses his legs like he's sitting on invisible ground and steeples his fingers under his lips. "I know of a way to make you fly. But you're with my enemy. Why should I help you?"

"Because I have something you want," I answer for Angel.

Peter's gaze slides to me and he drops lower. Taking a wide stance on the railing again, he places his hands to his hips. "And just what would that be, Hook?"

My jaw set, I reach under my collar and pull out the key. With a jerk, I tear the chain. The sun reflects in the metal as it's lying in my open palm. A sly grin creeps to Peter's lips. His fingers twitch and he flies closer, but I close my fist around the little key before he can grab it. "I want your word that you'll help Angel."

"What's my word to you, pirate?" he spits.

I wait until he looks me in the eyes and finally say in a severe tone, "Give me your word as my brother and I'll trust you."

Indecision fights with avarice in his eyes. He wants the key, even if all this is still just a stupid game for him. But he also cares for Angel—so much I can tell by his look. "All right. As your brother I promise to make Angel fly before night falls," he says. "If she can't go home then, I still get to keep the key."

Angel throws an uneasy glance at me. Is she worried she won't make it that fast? I close my fingers tighter around her hand, assuring her with a nod. She can do it. The only problem is I was hoping to get another day with her. One more night. Just a few hours where I could have her to myself and hold her.

But this is more important than what I want. We both nod at the same time, agreeing to Peter's terms.

"Okay. Come here, Angel, and bring the key," Peter orders, now wearing his stupid grin again. "I'll take you to the jungle. We'll train there."

"What? No," she protests and steps closer to me. "Why can't we train here?"

"Because you need pixie dust to fly." He reaches in his pockets and turns them from the inside out, making a wry face. "And I don't have any on me."

"Bring the pixie here then," I growl. "I guarantee that no one on board will harm her."

"Right. Tell us another!" Peter laughs and glides a few inches upward. "She's young, but she's not stupid. She'll never come to your ship."

"Then I'll accompany Angel."

The laugh ebbs out of Peter's throat. "I'll take *her* with me, not you."

I wrap my arm around Angel's shoulders and tuck her to my side. "If she goes, I go."

Peter watches with hawk-like eyes as I slide the key into my pocket. "Fine. I'll see what I can do about it. But if Tameeka comes, the Lost Boys will follow. You better take the ship back to the shore. Anchor at Mermaid Lagoon. We'll be there in an hour."

I don't wait until Peter flits away but turn around and yell the command to berth the Jolly Roger at Mermaid Lagoon. If Peter really wants to put his fingers on the key to the chest, he'd better be punctual—and bring a pixie.

I'm not giving up the chance to destroy this freaking watch and break the spell for nothing. I want Angel safely home by the end of the day. And afterward I just want to drown myself in the shark-polluted waters.

Chapter 12

Jamie stands by the railing, hands braced on the wood. Every few minutes, he glances at the sky then checks the coast for anyone approaching. I near him and stroke his back. He doesn't turn, but he wraps his arm around my shoulders and tucks me to his side.

"What's up with you?" I ask and tilt my head, searching his face.

"Nothing."

"You seem restless."

He releases a deep sigh. "I'm just trying to keep myself occupied so I don't think of the end of today." His eyes find mine. After a forced brief smile, he kisses my brow.

"Yes, me too," I whisper. Even though I'm happy to have finally found a way to get home and see my sisters again, I know I'm going to miss Jamie on a level that'll leave me hurting for a long time. But I've stayed here long enough. There's a life outside Neverland waiting for me. I have to go.

The cry of an eagle in the distance makes us both turn east. Peter is coming. And with him, holding onto his hand, is Tameeka, the fair-haired pixie.

"Let the Lost Boys come on board," Jamie calls out to Smee who then extends the gangplank together with Fin Flannigan. "Remember what I told you. These are exceptional circumstances. No one's going to kill Peter or the boys...today."

An agitated growl rumbles through the crew. They aren't happy with the situation, but they'd never rebel against their captain. And since I've been officially called the captain's girl after we returned from the lagoon this morning, they're all willing and some of them even happy to help me. I know this because Jack Smee subtly nods at me as Jamie and I wait to see our guests aboard. He even gives me the hint of an encouraging smile.

I'm being social with pirates. Who would have ever thought?

Skippy, Toby, Loney, Stan and Sparky file on deck and huddle together with the gangway behind them. It must feel weird to be on a pirate ship of their own free will. However free that will really was, I'll probably never know.

Stan runs the zipper of his bear-fur vest up and

down. When I catch his eyes, his cheeks flush pink. "Hey, Angel," he mumbles. "It's good to see you again. And alive, too."

"Hi, Stan," I reply and give him a true smile.

Rubbing the back of his neck, he lowers his gaze to the floorboards. "I'm sorry I didn't help you in the jungle."

"Forget about it. There's nothing you could have done." And to assure him I really mean it, I close the two steps between us and hug him. When I pull away, he's grinning like a raccoon. "What is it?" I demand.

The red in his cheeks intensifies. "You look like a girl."

"Yeah," Skippy seconds him, scratching his big left ear. "The dress looks much better on you than those fancy pants you wore last time."

Behind me, Jamie laughs softly and I cast a glance over my shoulder. "You so agree with that, don't you?" His laugh ebbs to a smirk. I'm totally in love with that devious half-smile.

When I turn back, Peter and Tami land by the boys. The sight of the pixie gives my heart a twinge. She reminds me so much of my little sisters. Longing overtakes me. I'm ready to start learning. I want to go home.

Tami's gaze meets mine for a long moment. Last time we met, she ran screaming from me because she thought I was a pirate. What does she think now that I'm holding Captain Hook's hand? Slowly, the corners of her mouth curl up. "Hello, Angel," she says in her bell-like voice. "I didn't think we would meet again. Peter was driving us all crazy talking about nothing but you. Well, Peter and Stan that is." She cuts a look to the boys and everyone laughs. I didn't think Stan could blush even more, but I was totally wrong. He's glowing like a tomato right now.

I tilt my head and send Peter a puzzled glance. He shrugs. It's good to see he wasn't so mad as to *not* talk about me. "Thanks for coming," I tell them all.

Peter nods. Then he holds out his hand to Jamie, and I almost think he wants him to shake it. But of course, Jamie pulls the key from his pocket and places it on Peter's palm. "You better stick to your word, little brother," he says.

"And you better find a crew that doesn't stink so bad," Peter replies with a mocking grimace.

I giggle but stop immediately at Jamie's low growl. "What?" I whisper. "He has a point."

Peter claps his hands, drawing our attention. "Now that everyone is here and all is settled, shall we begin?"

A rush of excitement comes over me. "I'm ready."

"Good. First you need to know the basics." He grabs Tami and me by the wrists and leads us to the middle of the deck, shooing a couple of mean-faced pirates away. "It takes two things to fly. First, you have to find the happiest thought in your mind and concentrate on it. I'm warning you, hold on to it at all times. If you lose it, you'll fall."

"Happy thought, got it," I say and already know what it'll be for me, cutting a brief glance over Tami's head to Jamie. Nervously, I clasp my hands in front of my stomach. "What's the other thing?"

Peter waggles his brows. "Pixie dust." When he ruffles Tami's hair, a soft gold rain powders her shoulders and the floorboards at her feet. He catches some in his cupped hands and pours it over me. It smells of blackberries and honey and the dust makes me sneeze twice.

"All right. Now try to fly!"

I stare at his expectant eyes. "Just like that?"

"Yeah," he assures me. "Just like that." With a small push of his legs, he lifts up in the air. It looks so easy when he does it.

Full of enthusiasm and thinking of the last time Jamie kissed me, I bend my knees slightly and push, taking a small jump forward. But instead of sailing up to the sky, I land on my feet again. I try flapping my arms up with the next little jump, again, and again, skipping around the Lost Boys until I'm back in my original position.

My shoulders slump and my mouth curls to a pout.

"Maybe you need more pixie dust," Peter suggests and ruffles Tami's hair again. When this still seems too little for him, he scoops the pixie up by her feet and flies with her over me. He shakes her face-down over my head. Shrieking and laughing at the same time, Tami protests, but he ignores her until her dress of ivy leaves falls down to her chest, revealing her white panties. The crew and the Lost Boys laugh and whistle.

"Put me down, Peter!" Tami scolds and he sets her back to her feet.

I catch Jamie's grin behind her. "You look like a marigold," he tells me. With all the pixie dust on my dress I do indeed.

I try another jump, but when that doesn't work either, Peter takes both my hands and lifts me up with him. "Now if this isn't enough, I don't know what to do with you."

There's no time for me to say anything, because the next instant he releases my wrists. A gasp escapes me as I plummet six feet down. Jamie catches me, holding me flush to his body. He gazes into my eyes and teases, "You wanna do that again?"

"No!"

With a thump, Peter lands beside us. "Seriously, Angel. With all that pixie dust you should be able to fly to the moon and back."

I grimace. "You think something is wrong with me?"

"Not with you, but maybe with your happy thought. What did you pick?"

Heat creeps to my cheeks. I'd rather not tell in front

of them all. But the smirk on Jamie's face confirms *he* knows. "Maybe thinking of me doesn't make you happy enough?" he purrs in my ear.

He was only joking, but there's something true about what he said. My face falls. "You're right," I whisper. Whenever I looked at Jamie in the past hour, my heart ached with longing for him. "Soon I'll be leaving Neverland, and then I'll never see you again. How can that be a happy thought?"

His eyes narrow, but I know he understands me. "Maybe you should pick something that you can look forward to then. Like your home. Or—"

"The twins," I finish for him and a smile already tugs on my lips. Their laughter chimes out in my mind, filling my chest with warmth. When I close my eyes, I think I only have to reach out and I can touch them. Paulina and the fairy bug. If I do this right, I'll see them in just a little while.

Loud cheering and whistling suddenly sounds from all directions. As I open my eyes again, Jamie is sinking to his knees in front of me—or so I assume at first when I look down at him. The truth is I started to levitate by only thinking of my baby sisters. Jamie smiles and pulls at my ankle when I drift away from him. "Not so fast, young lady. You train on the ship. As long as you don't know how to control...this"—he gestures up and down with his other hand—"I don't like you going overboard."

ANNA KATMORE

I nod and try to hold onto this special thought that makes me fly. Peter glides to my side and explains how to steer in the air. "You do the same thing as when you walk in a different direction. You just"—he shrugs—"change direction."

At a slow speed, I circle around Jamie twice then again in the other direction. "Okay, I think I got that. Now how do I speed up?"

"Will yourself forward."

I don't know how. Rowing with my arms doesn't get me anywhere. Neither does pedaling with my feet.

"With your thoughts you control your body. With your mind you just give a little *push*." On the last word, Peter pushes me in the back and I zoom across the decks, aiming straight at the door of Jamie's quarters.

"Oh no!"

"Go up!" Peter tells me, flying next to me. "Lift your head, look up, and then follow that direction!"

I do. And all of a sudden, the door is gone and so is the entire ship. There's only a never-ending blue sky ahead and the wind slaps in my face. "Woo-hoo!" I laugh out loud and twist in the air.

Peter keeps close to my side the whole time. His eyes shine with pride. It's infectious. "I did it!" I shout and spin again.

"Yes! Yes! But this is only the beginning. Now we need to work on your skills some more. Come down with me and take care that you aren't losing your happy thought."

Following him down to the tiny dot that is the Jolly Roger, I concentrate on Paulina and Brittney Renae's laugh. It's easy enough. Like they're calling me home.

In front of Jamie's quarters, I find him talking to Smee and holding something out to him on his palm. Something tiny. I can't see what it is, but they seem engaged deep in conversation. With a quick turn just above the floorboards, I sail over and grab Jamie's hat.

"Hey," he calls after me and laughs. "Give that back, you...thief!"

Landing on deck, I put the hat on my head and walk over to Jamie. On tiptoes, I look him in the eyes. "Pirate," I correct him and smirk.

He removes my hat, pursing his lips in a mocking manner. "Absolutely."

When Peter calls to teach me the finer arts of flying, Jamie presses a quick kiss on my cheek. "Have fun. I need Smee to help me with something in my study. See you in half an hour."

I nod and hurry to Peter. He tells me to find my happy thought again and lift up a few feet. Then he has me mirroring his moves. Left, right, left, up, down, left, up, a twist and a somersault. It's fun. I shoot up a little higher to pirouette and dance some more. Then I race Peter around the ship. He's enjoying this as much as I am.

We zoom up and down, back and forth. I feel safer with every passing minute. Shaking with laughter, I glide so close above the waves that I can see my happy reflection on the glistening surface. Water splashes left and right as I lower my hand and cut through it.

Going up again, I see how Brant Skyler sneaks up behind Tami with an excited grin, grabs her shoulders and shakes her so quickly that golden dust rains down from her hair. He cups some in Fin Flannigan's leather hat and pours it all over himself. Then he takes a few pixie-like jumps, dancing like an ugly-as-heck ballerina around the ship. Not flying but drifting really far on his jumps, he looks like he's having the time of his life. Tami gives him a mean pixie-scowl and shakes her finger at him.

It makes me laugh out louder. Flying is a thrill that shoots through my body in waves. I grin at Peter and nod my head at the sea. He takes on the challenge with a glint in his eyes and we race toward the horizon. When I look down, I see Melody zooming through the water like a dolphin beneath me. A moment later she whips out of the waves, jumping a few feet up, and we high-five each other before she drops and dives again. Her water fountain gets me in the face. Flying is heady! Never do I want to stop.

"We have a natural talent here," Peter cheers next to me. "I think you're ready. If you go like this, I'm sure you'll find home."

I nod and we return to the Jolly Roger. "Will you fly

with me?" I ask him.

"I can come for a bit. A few miles, probably, but not all the way."

We sink to the quarter deck. Smee is outside now, obviously finished with whatever Jamie wanted done. Next to him is Loney, with his hands shoved into his pockets. He grins up at Smee and pokes him in the ribs with his elbow. "Didn't ever think we'd become friends one day, eh?"

Jack Smee gazes straight ahead as he pulls out his sword and sets the blade flat against Loney's throat. "The captain said no killing the boys," he states in an indifferent voice. "He didn't say no cutting out their tongues if they get annoying."

Loney gulps and eases a few steps away from Smee and out of his sword's reach. It makes me giggle to watch Smee sheathe the sword again and direct a smug grin to no one in particular.

Looking for Jamie, I turn and find him right behind me. His hands are clasped behind his back. "So, you're ready to go now?" He's smiling, but I know it's forced.

I shrug and grimace. "I guess."

Taking a deep breath, he reaches for my hand and leads me to the rest of the crew and Peter's friends. "You probably want to say goodbye to some of them."

Since I don't know most of the pirates very well, I just wave at them and tell them thanks for not killing me.

But I shake hands with Jack Smee and I hug the tall and skinny Potato Ralph. He smells of onions and bacon.

Then I turn to the Lost Boys and Tami. The pixie grabs both my hands and flaps her butterfly wings until we're at eye level. "Have a safe journey home, Angel!" she wishes me and smiles bright like only a fairy-tale creature can do. Shaking her head, she powders me in an extra layer of pixie dust. As she flitters away, I step up to Loney.

He remains silent, but he hugs me tight, then he hands me on to Skippy, Toby, and Sparky. Last in line is Stan. "You were the best Lost Girl we ever had," he says with a sad pout.

"Because I was the *only* Lost Girl you ever had," I state and manage to tease a smile out of him. Then I kiss his cheek and wave at them all as they leave the ship on the gangplank leading to the shore. Peter is the only one who stays on board.

"Are you ready?" he asks me.

"Not quite." I turn around and catch Jamie's eyes across the deck. Not tearing my gaze away from him, I tell Peter, "Give me a minute with the captain then we can go."

Jamie is waiting for me by the wooden boxes. Slowly, I walk up to him, feeling how my happy thought slips away the farther I go. When I stand in front of him and he looks down at me with sad eyes, giant fists seem to squeeze my chest.

"Well, I guess this is it," I mumble.

He nods and draws in a deep breath. "This is it."

"I want to thank you, Jamie. I know what you're giving up so I can go home."

"Ah, it's okay. I've been living to find this goddamn treasure and the watch for so long, a few more years won't kill me." Rolling his eyes, Jamie shrugs. "Peter doesn't know what to do with the watch. I only have to find it *and* the key now."

"Yeah. A never-ending game, huh?"

He chuckles and graces my jaw with his knuckle. "That's what Neverland is, love."

His last word makes me smile. "Don't be too hard on Peter," I tell him.

Jamie waves it off. "Ah, he can handle it."

It feels like we're talking about trivial things, just to avoid speaking the one word we both dread. Goodbye.

A moment later Jamie's eyes turn serious. "It's time. You should be going now so you get home before you fall asleep and forget everything again."

I nod. Then I hug myself because I know if I touch him now, tears will spill over and I won't be able to make them stop.

"But before you leave, I have something for you." He reaches into his chest pocket and pulls out a tiny red thing on a silver chain.

"The ruby," I breathe. Somehow he managed to drill

a tiny hole through the gem and threaded the chain through. I wonder if this was what he was doing with Smee in his study while I learned to fly.

"It's not much. The only thing that I have left of my treasure." Jamie places the ruby heart on my bare skin and fastens the link behind my neck. "But I guess it's enough for you to remember us by. Me. The pirates. And Peter," he adds with a playful grunt and rolls his eyes. Then he takes my face between his hands and touches his forehead to mine. "It was a pleasure to have you on board, *Fancy-pants* Angelina McFarland."

Reaching up for his arms, I giggle, though I don't feel like giggling at all. I feel like I'm breaking apart.

"Okay. And now…think a happy thought." With that he touches his lips very gently to mine. I wrap my arms around him and he crushes me to his chest for a long moment. Then he lets go and I step away.

Peter lands on the railing next to me. He holds out his hand and helps me up. When I sigh and turn to look out at the horizon, my chest aches so bad that I think there are stones inside that will pull me underwater as soon as I take a step forward, off the railing.

"A happy thought, Angel," Jamie says softly behind me. He skims his fingers over the back of my hand. I don't turn around to him. I can't. From the deepest part of my heart, I pull the thought of my sisters' laughter and wait until the lightness of before comes over me again. Then I slowly lift into the air with Peter by my side.

"I'll miss you, Jamie," I say. But I don't look back.

James Hook

I don't know how long I stand by the railing and watch the sky that has swallowed the only girl that I have ever felt something for. Every time I think of her name, of her soft hand on my cheek or even just her gentle voice, an invisible sword pierces my heart anew. It feels like I'm bleeding to death from the pain.

"Cap'n, the crew wants to know when we're setting sail again."

I turn around to Jack. His face is grave. Although he doesn't experience the pain I'm feeling, he understands. Placing a hand on my shoulder, his eyes fill with empathy. "It's best for the lass, you know," he says.

I nod and step away from the railing. "We've anchored long enough! Put her out, ye scabby rats!" I bark at the crew. Only my voice breaks midsentence. I can't get rid of the bile in my throat. Pinching the bridge of my nose, I tell Smee through clenched teeth, "Take over."

When he's gone, driving the men to set sail and steer

the ship out of Mermaid Lagoon, I slump down by the wooden boxes, lean back and gaze at the sky. Here I kissed Angel for the first time. A sad smile tugs at the corners of my mouth. Blow me down, it was a mighty fine kiss.

As the captain of the Jolly Roger, I should get over myself and be a man again. A pirate. Their commander, goddammit. But I just don't want to leave this spot. Not yet. Maybe in an hour or two. Or maybe I'll just sit here and watch the sky the entire night. After all, I have all the time in Neverland, don't I? And I'll spend it alone. Well, with a crew of sixteen pirates and a handful of rats in the bilge.

Breathing deep, I put on my hat. I'd taken it off before Angel came to say goodbye. She should remember me as *just Jamie* and not the ruthless pirate she'd gotten to know first.

I rub my hands over my face and sigh as, in the sky, two dots appear at the horizon. They are growing bigger. Gripped by strange excitement, I sit straight and narrow my eyes to make out what's coming toward us. Holy hell, is it Angel and Peter? What if she changed her mind? I jump to my feet and cross to the railing, leaning out far. The small spots come nearer and nearer. I can barely breathe.

Moments later, the things in the sky become a pair of seagulls that sail over the ship on the breeze. I angle my head and follow their path to the shore. My heart sinks. I fall to my knees. It's over. Angel is gone. She won't come back.

Chapter 13

The laughter of two little girls. That's what keeps me going on through the sky with my arms spread-eagle and my gaze strictly focused frontward. Peter and I glide through a layer of clouds, climbing higher and higher. Neverland is now a small spot in the ocean behind us.

After everything I've seen and gone through the past few days, nothing will ever amaze me again. And still, here I fly and can't believe it. This is the most unlikely thing I could ever imagine doing...apart from kissing a pirate.

"So, you and Hook, huh?" Peter asks after some time of silently gliding next to me.

Cutting him a brief glance, I purse my lips. What'll his next comment be? That I couldn't sink any lower than making out with a pirate?

Peter startles me. "You're good for him. I've never seen him act so...*human*. It's a shame you're leaving."

I turn to him again, but this time he keeps his attention focused in front and ignores my baffled stare. Maybe he enjoyed the afternoon on board the Jolly Roger. It must have been a great experience to work with and not against his own brother for the first time in his life.

I only wish they'd find a way of keeping this up after I'm gone. But then, what's it to me, really? I'll never find out once I'm back. I mean, it's not like I can grab my phone and call Jamie to check in on him.

A sad feeling claws at my heart at the memory of our last real kiss. The one we shared at Mermaid Lagoon at night. His scent of tangerines and seawater has seeped into my pores and settled in my heart. It will remain with me always. If only he could kiss me just one more time. Or hold me like he did when we said goodbye. I miss him, and part of me wants to turn around and fly back into his arms.

As if I'd hit an air hole, I drop three feet. Gasping, I struggle to gain control and plummet another couple of feet. Peter's arm is around me in an instant. "Angel," he yells through the wind. "Where's your happy thought?"

Gone for a careless moment.

From the depth of my heart I pull Paulina's laugh and Brittney Renae's giggle. "I'm all right. You can let go," I tell Peter.

He eyes me with skepticism, but eventually he pulls his arm away from my waist. Still, his gaze remains on me like that of a hawk. I try to ban Jamie from my thoughts altogether and save thinking of him for later. When I'm home.

We fly for what feels like hours in the same direction. The sky doesn't change. Neither does the dark blue sea beneath us. It's impossible to say how far Tameeka's pixie dust will carry me—if I'll make it to London after all or just plummet to the waves at some point. Peter has come with me way farther than I expected.

"Shouldn't you return to Neverland?" I ask him.

He arches a brow at me. "And risk you losing your happy thought again? I don't think so."

"But you can't come with me the entire way, can you?"

"I'll have to." He laughs and it sounds as carefree as ever. "Hook has been after my life for a long time. But if I let something happen to you on this journey, he's going to *really* kill me. So just concentrate on whatever keeps you up in the clouds with me and we're both going to be okay."

His bright spirit cheers me up. I enjoy the idea of having company for the rest of the way. And then I see it. There's land ahead. "Peter!" I gasp and point down to the green spot that flashes between the clouds.

"I see it too!" He takes my hand and pulls me on a little faster, already descending.

So this is it. This is *home*. My heart clops like a

racing horse. In just a few minutes I'll be with my family again. What will the twins say? Oh, I can't wait...

At a killer speed, we dive through the clouds. The sun stands lower now and casts a dreamy glow on the island and the ocean around it.

Island? *Wait.* I know London is located on an island too, but this one beneath us looks too darn familiar. It's shaped like a half moon.

Peter seems to realize where we are at the same time, because he pulls me to a hover in the air. When he looks at me, his eyes are wide with shock and sorrow.

"How can this be, Peter?" I plead. "We've never changed direction and we've gone so far!"

His face scrunches in mournful lines as he shrugs, forlorn. "It seems like Neverland doesn't want to let you go."

Remembering what Jamie showed me on the map of Neverland the other day after we returned from the sailing trip, I wonder if the same happened today. Did Peter and I fly around the globe where Neverland is located? Is it really a small star and not just a place you can fly away from?

With all my hope, my happy thought slips away from me. Suddenly I have no grip on the air anymore but only dangle from Peter's hand that is tightly wrapped around my wrist. He pulls me to his chest and sinks toward Neverland. Tears are battling to the surface of my eyes.

For a brief moment I wonder if Peter will take me to his tree house in the jungle, but as we're headed toward the shore on the west side and the sails of the Jolly Roger come into view, it's clear he knows where I want to go.

He lands on deck and releases me. Every pirate on board gapes at us, open-mouthed. Even Jack Smee's eyes are wider than saucers. But the only one I want to see right now is sitting on the pile of wooden boxes and gazing out to the sea. Knees pulled to his chest, he's resting his arms on them. The big black hat dipped forward, there's a sad tilt to his head.

Breaking away from Peter, I run to Jamie. He straightens at my footsteps on the floorboards and jerks around. In another second he is on his feet and wraps me in his tender embrace. "Angel, what the— You're back!" He pushes me away from him to look at my face. There's wonder and confusion in his eyes. "Blow me down, why did you— Ah, Angel!" Crushing me to his chest again, he strokes his hand over my hair and neck. He wants to laugh and I think he wants to cry at the same time. But he's too startled to even get a complete sentence out of his mouth.

Moving my arms around him, I dig my fingers into his shirt at his back and bury my face against his chest. "Flying didn't work," I sob.

"What?" He holds me away from him once more and brushes the hair out of my face with both hands. "How could it not?"

"I don't know."

"We went straight north all the time," Peter explains from behind me. "But somehow we reached Neverland from the south again."

"It's like when we went out with the Jolly Roger," Jamie concludes in a flat voice. But then another rush of excitement shakes him. "You're back!" He sighs and hugs me so tight, all the air whizzes out of my lungs. "We'll find another way," he promises after a tender kiss to my brow. "Don't you worry, we *will* send you home."

I lean into him and know he won't rest until I'm back at my house in London. But for now, he's just happy to see me. And I to see him.

"What do you think went wrong?" he asks over my head.

Turning to the other side, I see Peter shrug. "Maybe we didn't go up high enough. But seriously, I have no idea." Then he narrows his eyes and steps closer.

A queer tension grips me. "What?" Jamie and I ask at once.

"You said you can leave Neverland only the same way you came here, right?"

My brows knit together like his as I nod. "Why?"

"Angel, you didn't *fly* to Neverland." His voice drops to an ominous level. "You fell."

Oh my God. The air freezes in my lungs. He's right.

"So there's really no way for me to leave this world—"
Lips trembling, my voice breaks on the last words.

Peter grimaces. "I wouldn't exactly say that."

"What do you mean?"

"Basically, that you just have to fall off somewhere to get back. But I don't think a knee-high chair will do."

All my hope is tied to Peter's idea. "Then what do you suggest?"

The guys exchange uncomfortable glances then Jamie asks me, "How high was that balcony you dropped from?"

It was on the second floor. A glance around the ship and the lowest mast comes into focus. I point my finger at it. "About as high as that." Jamie's grumble as he contemplates it draws my attention. My eyes dry as they widen in understanding. "You're not expecting me to throw myself down from a mast?"

He rubs his nape and shakes his head. "Not from this one. The boxes beneath would shorten your fall." He pauses. "We're going up there." With a nod to the side he indicates the mast in the middle of the deck. The highest one. With nets attached to climb up and several crosspieces.

My throat is tight. "And just how high do you want me to climb?" From the look on Jamie's face I get that he intends to go up all the way. Lips compressed, I nod, resigned. If their plan doesn't work, I'm going to be mash on the main deck. "Just great."

ANNA KATMORE

"Don't worry. I'll come up with you, Angel." Jamie takes my hand, kisses my knuckles and pulls me against him. "And Peter will wait down here to catch you if anything goes wrong."

Peter coughs. It's one of those scary coughs that tell you in an instant that you missed something essential. Something that might take your life if you're stupid enough to ignore it.

"What?" I drawl, fighting these creepy misgivings.

"It might not work if I catch you before the impact. I really think you have to go through with it. And Angel—"

"What? There's more?" I blurt, almost hysterical now.

"You'll have to wash off all the pixie dust, too."

"There's a snag in everything, huh?" Laughing when you don't in the least feel like doing so is a weird thing. I can't stop, until it turns into sobbing and Jamie hugs me to his chest.

"Shh," he soothes me. "It'll be all right. You can do this."

He leads me into his quarters where I go to the primitive bathroom for another shower—hopefully my last one in Neverland. Using only one bucket of water this time, I save the other for washing all the pixie dust out of the dress. Done with that, I slip into a shirt Jamie gave me. The white linen clings to my wet skin and reaches to the middle of my thighs. The wide collar slips off one shoulder as I head out of the bathroom.

In the doorway to the quarter deck, Potato Ralph waits for me to hand him my wet dress. He offered to dry it over the stove in the galley for me. Jamie closes the door behind him then turns to me, his gaze roaming over my body from my eyes to my naked toes and back. I'm just standing there in the middle of his room, feeling cold and scared of what's still to come tonight.

"Can I get you something?" he asks after some time. "Something to drink or—"

"How about some of the rum you drank the other night?" I kid with little amusement.

Surprised, he tilts his head and arches his brows at me. He looks sweet and makes me smile. "Never mind," I say and shake my head. Not knowing what else to do, I climb onto his bed and pull my knees to my chest, hugging my thighs beneath them.

His hat dangling from his hand now, Jamie comes over and sits in front of me, one leg tucked underneath him, the other foot still on the floor.

"When Peter and I returned and saw you on deck, you seemed sad," I say after a while of silently staring into his shiny blue eyes.

There's no change in his serious but soft expression. "I wasn't sad. I—" His gaze drops to my feet and after a moment lifts to my face again. His eyes fill with ache. "When you were gone, Angel, I hit rock bottom."

A warmth crawls over me. I don't know if it comes from his words or from his tender fingers that just curled around my ankles. His thumbs begin to stroke my skin.

"You know that you didn't have to tell me about my past. You could have kept it a secret from me and made me stay with you," I argue.

It's a stupid thought and it shouldn't have even entered my mind, but when I find myself lost in his touch, I wonder if after today I could be happy in Neverland forever. Jamie is a temptation I didn't reckon with in my struggle to find home. All these feelings confuse me and I shake my head. "I—I thought that you…"

"That I like you? That I *love* you?" A slow smile curves his lips. "By now you should know that it's all true." His lids at half-mast, he reaches for my hands and places a sweet kiss to my knuckles. Long, honey-colored lashes blink open. His mouth is still on my skin when he whispers, "And I guess it's safe to assume you feel the same way about me."

I do.

Jamie straightens again and moves a little closer, taking both my ankles and gently lifting my legs to rest them over his thigh. I brace myself on the mattress. One of his hands slides over mine, the other lifts to the back of my neck.

My eyes averted, I see our shadows dance on the wall in the candlelight. They are nearing each other. Angling his head, Jamie brushes his lips over the corner of my mouth. The kiss is so light, it causes the little hairs at the back of my neck to bristle.

As if he knows exactly what he is doing to me, he does it again. This time, I can feel him smile. Or smirk? He sure enjoys my reaction to him. I don't let him tease me any longer but tilt my head at the third caress. Briefly he stops, his eyes shining warm in the candlelight. Then he molds his mouth to mine.

At his gentle pressure, I open my mouth. Our lips barely touch when our tongues do. The world starts to spin around me, and I close my eyes to shut it out. Jamie is the only one I let in. For all I know, this will be our last real kiss.

James Hook

Angel's leg is draped over my hip, her cheek pillowed against my chest as she dozes. Not a good idea, given that in her sleep she'll most likely forget everything I told her today. Her dress might have dried by now, but I can't find it in my heart to drag her back to reality. *My* reality, not hers.

The candle on the small table by the door has burned down to half its size. The flame's soft glow fills my room with peace and so do Angel's content breaths. Carefully, I pull the blanket farther up her back and caress the downy skin on her neck. The scent of tangerine drifts from her hair and tempts me to press a kiss to the top of her head. I don't want to let her slip away from me just yet.

"Your heart is beating so slowly, I thought you were asleep," Angel says in a soft voice.

Tilting my head back, I smile as I study the ceiling and the many knotholes in the wood. "I thought the same about you."

"No, I was just listening to that beautiful sound. Beat, beat, pause...beat, beat, pause..." She shifts on me so her chin is pressing into my sternum and grins. "I could listen to it all night."

I rake my fingers through her hair. "Nice idea. Need I remind you that we have other plans, though?"

"Maybe I changed my mind? Don't you want me to stay? In Neverland? On this ship?" A dauntless gleam enters her eyes. "With you?"

"Ah, Angel. I wish I could keep you with me forever." She's holding my heart in a tight grip. The thought of having her on the Jolly Roger and being able to steal a fevered kiss like the one twenty minutes ago whenever I want is tempting as hell. I want to keep her with me, because after the past few days, I know that I'm hopelessly in love with this girl. "Remember what you asked the other night?" I say quietly. "What my biggest adventure was?"

She gives a slight nod.

"There was a time when I spent many afternoons with the fairies. Bre'Shun and I philosophized the hours away. One day she asked me what I thought would be the biggest adventure of all time. I said to be a pirate and find the biggest treasure out there." Skimming the bangs out of Angel's eyes, I keep back a smile. "She laughed at me then."

"What did she think it was?" Angel asks.

ANNA KATMORE

"Bre said there's only one *real* adventure in this world. Love. It's finding the one person who makes you want to be better than you are."

Angel's eyes shine warmer as a smile plays on her lips. "You didn't believe her?"

"No, I didn't." I kiss the tip of her nose. "Now I know she was right. And by the way you look whenever I do this"—I brush my thumb across her cheekbone and Angel squeezes her eyes shut, leaning into my palm—"I can tell how much you enjoy being with me, too. I really wish it was enough for you, Angel. Me. The pirate life I can offer you. And Neverland. But there are two girls waiting for you somewhere." A sigh escapes me. "And you love them more than me."

Her grin slips away. "No, Jamie, it's not true," she whispers, but she knows I'm right. And we better get through what we have to do, before one of us forgets about it and makes a stupid decision. It's not unlikely that it'll be me.

"I'm going to get your dress." Gently easing her off of me, I roll to the side and get out of my bed. On the floor at the end of the bed, my discarded boots wait for me. I pull them on then walk out the door to retrieve Angel's gown from the galley.

Sidelong glances follow me across the decks. On the highest mast above even the crow's nest, Peter lounges on the crosspiece, legs stacked in the net and arms folded behind his head. He looks like he's taking a nap up there. When I stop to zoom in on him, he casts me a slanted look from under the mud-brown leather hat he doubtlessly stole from Fin Flannigan.

For all it's worth, I don't mind him still hanging out on my ship. In fact, it gives me a kind of reassuring feeling to have him there when Angel is going to take a jump off the mast in a little while. Breaking our locked gaze, I stride under deck and find the galley empty. All the better. Clipped to a line above the stove, her dress hangs like a blackjack that's lost its wind. The smell of cooked food clings to the fabric, but it could be worse. It's a good thing Angel washed her dress with soap earlier.

I pull it down and bring it back to my room. Angel is sitting on the edge of my bed, still wearing my shirt. I toss the dress into her arms then give her a private moment to change. When she's done, she comes up behind me as I stand in front of my wardrobe buttoning up a fresh shirt that I just put on...because I didn't know what else to do. Her soft hands roam up my back. In spite of the warmth it evokes inside me, her touch makes me sad. I turn around. "Are you ready to go?" *Home...*

Angel nods. I take her hand and plant a kiss into her palm. Then I pick up my hat from the floor. Her mouth curls disapprovingly. I quickly kiss the pout away before I put on my hat.

Together we walk through the door, more stones

weighing down my heart with every step. The entire crew has lined up by the railing, which surprises me. They tell Angel goodbye in their creepy pirate manner. Some of them even take down their hats. I grin to myself and shake my head as we pass each one.

Last in line is Smee. He's the only one who takes a step forward and places a gentle hand on her shoulder. "Good luck, Angel," he says, inclining his head. Heck, he means it. They all mean it. As their captain for countless decades I've never been this impressed.

And Angel too, it seems. "Thank you, Jack," she tells him and smiles. "Take good care of the captain, will you?"

Smee cuts a glance at me, which I return with rolling my eyes. As if I needed someone to look after me. But it's nice to hear her worrying nevertheless.

Then we start to climb. I let Angel go first. It's a long way up to the top of the mast and I feel better right beneath her in case she loses her grip. Peter is already there and supports Angel on the crosspiece until I follow.

She hugs him tight and kisses his cheek as they say goodbye. It makes me grit my teeth but I give her the moment with her friend—my brother. Then she turns to me.

For an endless moment we just look into each other's eyes. Bile rises in my throat. Probably in hers, too, because she swallows hard and her lips start to tremble. I reach out and caress her cheek. "No tears. Not tonight," I whisper.

"Let me remember you with a smile, Angelina McFarland."

She sniffs and the corners of her mouth tilt up, but it's forced. Finding a hold on the net behind the crosspiece, she takes a cautious step toward me then flings her arms around my neck. I can't let go of the net, or we'd both tumble to the ground. It doesn't matter. I wrap my free arm around her waist and crush her to my chest. "I'll miss you," I breathe into her ear.

"Just don't forget me, Jamie."

"How could I ever?"

Against the skin on my neck I feel her tears. They break me. I reach for her chin and tilt her face up, brushing the wet trail on her cheek away with my thumb. Then I kiss her one last time. Only our lips touch for a long tender moment.

As she pulls away from me, I take off my hat and put it on her head. Now I get what I want—Angel's honest smile.

Peter leads her to the very edge of the crosspiece where she turns around to face me. Her mien is brave, but her eyes are filled with sadness. Slowly closing them, she takes a deep breath. I swallow against the pain in my throat. Then she tips backward and falls.

Gripping the net to my right, I rush forward and desperately cry out her name. But it's too late. Angel drops toward the sea beneath her. Her arms are stretched out at her sides and the skirt of her blue dress is flapping in the wind like it's waving goodbye. The pirate hat flies off her head. Swaying sadly, it follows in the wake of her fall.

A moment later, the love of my endless life submerges in the ocean.

I pray that she gets where she longs to be.

Chapter 14

A splash of water hits my face. I gasp for air. The waves should have swallowed me, but the ground beneath me is hard. I struggle to open my eyes. Someone is bent over me. Soft hands touch my cheeks. Blinking a few times, I only catch glimpses of a purple dress. "Bre'Shun?" I mumble.

"Oh no, she hit her head!" a familiar voice pipes out to my right. Too familiar...and it sounds wonderful! This time, in spite of the achy head, I put more effort into focusing. Then I see her. *Them.*

"Fairy bug!" Still on my back, I grab my little sister and pull her to my chest. Then I reach for Paulina and squeeze both of them so hard, the air wheezes out of their lungs.

Paulina wraps her tiny arms around my throat and buries her face in the crook of my neck. A relieved sigh

　　　　　　　　　　　ANNA KATMORE

escapes her. "We thought you were dead! You didn't answer for so long." She's almost crying. But I only laugh. I laugh so hard that the entire street should be able to hear me and hug them tighter. I never intend to let them go.

The twins help me sit up on the snow-covered ground. Water drips from the garden hose at Brittney Renae's feet and forms a puddle. "What did you do with the hose?" I ask.

"We splashed your face," Paulina informs me. Then her sweet little face crunches up in a grimace as though she expects to be scolded. "It was Brittney's idea. She said you would wake up then."

Well, this explains why I'm wet all over. I turn to Brittney Renae and ruffle her hair. "Great idea, fairy bug."

Giggling, she dances over to the tap and turns it off. Paulina pulls on my hands to make me get on my feet. This is the first time I realize I'm wearing my own clothes again. The jeans and my black tee. It isn't torn any longer.

I take a deep breath. Was it all just a dream? Everything about Neverland, about Peter Pan and…Jamie? With a jolt of shock, I remember which book I read with the girls before I fell. Could I really have hurt my head so badly that I dreamed up such a fantastic story?

Maybe. But the longing that seeps into my heart makes me believe otherwise. When I close my eyes, a roguish smirk is all I see. The scent of tangerine still lingers in my nostrils. Could it all really have just been a dream?

The pain in my chest is very real.

Where's my sweater? Looking around, I can't spot it anywhere. Maybe it snagged on the twigs when I fell. Lifting my head, I scan the tree, but it's too dark to make out anything.

Paulina tugs at my hand. When I look down at her happy face, she squeezes harder. "Can we go inside? It's so cold out here."

Brittney Renae grabs my other hand and we walk back into the house. The warmth floods me. It smells of cinnamon cookies that Miss Lynda smuggled in this afternoon. And of beech wood burning in the fireplace.

It smells of home.

Shivering, I send the girls to their rooms to change for bed then I hurry into the bathroom to get rid of my wet clothes. There's my pink bathrobe hanging from a hook on the inside of the door. Wrapped around me tightly, it warms my trembling body. I push my feet into the matching fluffy slippers and shuffle first to Brittney Renae's room to tuck her in. I kiss her goodnight and hug her for a long time.

Then I head for Paulina's room. After she fell asleep, I get up from her bed and skim my fingers over the book on her nightstand. *Peter Pan.* A flying kid is portrayed on the cover. My heart swells, the memory of him still vivid and warm in my mind.

I pick up the book and take it with me, turning off the honey bunny's light. Back in my own room, I sit on my bed and open the book. Tinker Bell, the Lost Boys, everyone's there. Even a white-haired Smee grins from the page. And next to him...Captain Hook. He wears that gaudy red brocade coat and black hat that Disney put him in. He looks so much different from the *original*. The real guy. Just Jamie.

My chest hurts awfully as I stroke my fingers over his face. Just a dream...was it really?

Sliding the book under my pillow, I get up and shrug out of the bathrobe. It lands in a pink heap on the floor next to my bed. From my closet, I fetch a short, satiny nightgown. It's not what I usually wear at night, but it was a present from my grandma a couple of years ago and ever since then it's waited on a hanger to be taken out and worn. I don't know why I want to put it on tonight of all nights. Maybe because the soft blue reminds me of what I've been wearing for the past few days. Because it reminds me of him...

I slip it over my head and walk to the mirror at my door. Held by thin satin straps, the dress hangs silky soft from my shoulders. My bare legs are white from the cold and my hair is a wet mess. But that's not the reason why I gasp right now.

A beautiful heart-shaped ruby rests against my cleavage, attached to a slender silver chain around my neck.

My lips start to tremble, as do my knees. The mirror fogs up with my fast breaths. Why? *How?* Skimming my fingers over the smooth facets of the shiny gem, I feel tears welling up in my eyes.

It's true! I was there.

With no idea what to really expect, I look down at my hand and twist it. There's half a tattoo on the inside. The letter A and some stars dusted beneath what once was the name *Angel.* Paulina gave it to me less than an hour ago. But during the past five days it has faded away.

I've met them all. Peter, Tami, the fairies. And James Hook. The most incredible man I've ever known. He sneaked into my heart in a real pirate manner. My throat constricts and hurts when I think of him.

There's a rap at my door just before the first tears would have spilled over. I clear my throat and open it. Paulina stands in the doorway with her stuffed bunny in her small arms. A single tear rolls down her cheek. "When I close my eyes, I see you lying in the garden. You don't answer to Brittney and me."

"Aw." I sink to my knees and brush her bangs off her forehead. "Everything is all right, honey bunny. I'm fine. You two brought me back."

"I know. But I don't want to see you lying on the ground when I cannot feel you. Can I sleep in your bed tonight?"

Smiling, I stand up and lift Paulina into my arms. I carry her to my bed, where she crawls under the duvet and grins at me from my pillow. After the light is out and I sneak under the covers, she snuggles up against my chest and her content sigh drifts to me. I kiss the top of her head with one arm wrapped tightly around her. My other hand moves up to the ruby heart. Closing my fingers around it, I shut my eyes and return to Neverland. Even if only in a dream...

Three months later...

Warm evening breeze plays around my bare ankles. The heels of my sandals clack on the concrete as I walk up the road to our house, stepping in and out of the wide circles of light the lamp posts cast on the street every fifty feet.

My parents walk a few steps in front of me, my father carrying a tired Brittney Renae. Her head rests sleepily on his shoulder, her arms hanging loosely at her sides. It's past ten o'clock in the evening. Paulina holds tight to my hand and tries to keep up with her small steps. The twins should have been put to bed hours ago. But a dinner party at my father's friend's house that dragged on too long prevented that from happening.

Gee, I'm tired of these banquets. Sitting straight through a meal that consists of more courses than any normal person should be forced to eat is always a challenge. No giggling, no murmuring, no swinging our legs under the table. These dinners usually make me feel like I'm in boot camp. If this is difficult for me, it must be pure torture for my little sisters. Sometimes, I wish the three of us could have grown up in a more adventurous place than the McFarland home. A place like—

Yeah, like what? Like Adventureland in Disney World? I sigh, studying the stars. They seem to beckon me with their shining light, and have done so for a while now. But I can't imagine how I'll ever get up there, so I guess I'll just have to put up with the fake smiles of adults and the gossip of people I don't know.

My life hasn't always been dreary like this. A few months ago, I felt different. A whole lot of different. It was connected to a red glass heart I wore on a necklace. One morning, I woke up in my bed and found my hand wrapped around it. But that wasn't the only strange thing that day. Paulina was curled up next to me as well. She never sleeps in my bed, so that was a surprise. When I nudged her and she opened her eyes, she sat up in a rush and hugged me with all the love of a five-year-old.

I'd hit my head, she told me then. Apparently I'd fallen off my balcony. It made sense, because I couldn't remember what had happened the night before. As for the heart pendant, Paulina said it wasn't from her, even though I was sure she'd gotten it as a free gift from one of her Disney magazines and slipped it around my neck while I slept.

I couldn't explain the feeling of longing that overcame me whenever I looked at the red heart. A big part of me wanted to be somewhere else. Maybe even *with* someone. A touch of homesickness filled me, one I couldn't figure out—because I was home. It weirded me out, so after some time, I took off the necklace and stored it at the back of a drawer in my desk with a stack of papers placed over it.

With the necklace out of sight, the longing faded. I could be my normal self again, in George and Mary McFarland's house.

Squeezing my little sister's hand as we step into another pool of light, I look down at her and know that it's a good place to be after all.

We pass our neighbor's garden. The scent of apple trees drifts to me. I lift my chin and breathe in deeply as something tugs gently at me... A memory? But I can't put the images together.

Then I see him.

A young man steps away from the shadows farther up the street and walks towards us. His head is lowered, the cap he wears covering his face from my view. The wide skate pants and the black hoodie he wears don't fit his determined, predatory strides.

I don't know why, but of all the people we pass, he's the only one who catches my attention. My parents obviously don't pay him any notice, and smoothly sidestep him. I want to do the same, but at that instant, he lifts his head and I find myself trapped in reckless blue eyes.

Familiar.

That strange feeling of homesickness stirs again. My heart decides to skip a couple of beats before it knocks savagely against my ribcage.

The guy's jaw is set, his gaze unwavering as he passes me. His warm fingers slip something into my hand. At the skin contact, a shiver races up my arm and makes me want to touch him again. I catch the scent of adventure on him—if adventure could have a smell—a whiff of seawater and tangerines. It intoxicates my mind and takes me away to a place I should know. A place behind those blue, blue eyes.

The piece of paper in my hand drags me out of my crazy thoughts.

Freezing on the spot, I pull Paulina to a halt with me and spin around. He doesn't stop, his resolute strides taking him fast down the street. I open my mouth and almost shout after him when he slides a glance over his shoulder and arches one challenging eyebrow. Moments later, he disappears into the shadows.

"What's wrong?" Paulina whispers to me.

Confused, I look down at her and shake my head. Then I stare at the note in my hand. With trembling fingers, I unfold it. The moonlight highlights the masculine scrawl:

Meet me on your balcony.

ANNA KATMORE

To be continued...

Finish this book with a song.

Dexter Britain – A Closing Statement

You can find it on YouTube

https://www.youtube.com/watch?v=IljIj1Q9cnI

Dear reader,

Please don't damn me for the cliffhanger. I know it's a mean moment to stop, but another book was the only possible way to fill the gap between Angel's fall and the last chapter. And I'm sure you all want to know what happened in Neverland after Hook and Angel said goodbye, don't you? ;-)

Be prepared for
PAN'S REVENGE

The adventure continues...

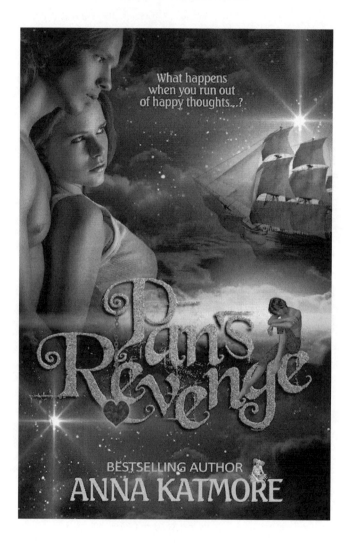

What happens
when you run out
of happy thoughts...?

Pan's Revenge

BESTSELLING AUTHOR
ANNA KATMORE

"Are you ready to be kissed?" he breathes against the corner of my mouth.

My knees start to tremble and there are butterflies in my belly now. Way too many. "I don't think this is a good idea."

"I think it's the best idea I've had in a long time."

Desperate to leave Neverland and find his love in this notorious town called London, James Hook makes a grave mistake. He puts his own wishes above those of his half-brother and once-arch-enemy, Peter Pan.

The consequences alter Peter's life in a way no one could have foreseen. The boy who wouldn't grow up swears revenge, and what better way than by stealing Hook's girl?

The first to arrive in London, Peter finds Angel once again without any memory of ever being in Neverland. That gives him time to plant the idea of a ruthless pirate captain in her mind—someone who tried to kill her once and is now on his way to kidnap her again. If only this stubborn girl would stop playing with Peter's head. He'd completely forgotten how beautiful she was. Or is it only because he sees her through *different* eyes now?

Through a shower of falling stars, a loop around the moon, and then a hard left at the Clock Tower—when James Hook finally arrives in London, he has to fight with a vengeance for his love and face a boy who grew up after all...

Playlist

Jonatha Brooke – Second Star To The Right
(Catching snow on the balcony)

Main Title of *Peter Pan*
(Falling)

Dexter Britain – The Time To Run
(Neverland Theme)

Birdy – Heart Of Gold
(Broken spirit)

Olly Murs – Ready for Love
(An argument)

Yiruma – Moonlight
(Just Jamie)

Ed Sheeran – I See Fire
(There's something about her)

Lifehouse – Everything
(Realizing he's going to miss her)

Tori Amos – China
(He wants to be selfish)

A Great Big World ft. Christina Aguilera – Say Something
(The biggest adventure)

A Fine Franzy – Blow Away
(With the right thought)

Poppy Girls – The Call
(Flying didn't work)

Theme of *The Little Mermaid*
(Falling again)

Dexter Britain – A Closing Statement
(He is here)

Don't miss Anna Katmore's amazing
teen romance PLAY WITH ME

ANNA KATMORE

Ryan Hunter's parties are legend.
And tonight she's going to be there.

Liza Matthews has been in love with her best friend since kindergarten. They're close as can be. They've even slept in each other's bed. But they've never kissed. Weeks away from her seventeenth birthday, Liza hopes that soon things will change between them. But when Tony comes home after summer soccer camp, his mind is focused on someone else. And worse, that new girl is a soccer player.

Fighting for her love, Liza gets carried away and makes a stupid decision: Without the least bit of talent or any passion for the sport whatsoever, she goes for the co-ed soccer team.

The tryouts are hell, the first match ends bloody, and the morning after the selection party she wakes up in the worst place possible—in the arms of the captain of the soccer team. The hottest guy in school. Ryan Hunter.

The sweet, hot and funny
Grover Beach Team series!
By Anna Katmore

*

Play With Me

Ryan Hunter

T Is For...

Kiss with Cherry Flavor

Dating Trouble

As usual in this place, I want to say thanks to a few awesome people out there.

Mom, Dad ... I love you. I don't know where I would be without your support and encouragement.

Johann and Kevin ... You two are my everything.

Silvia ... Thank you for dragging me away from my books whenever it gets too much and I need a break.

Lynda ... You know you're my online bestie, and I love you for the wonderful work you do in your critiques.

Jessa Markert ... Thanks for being a lovely beta-reader and giving me awesome feedback.

ANNA KATMORE

ABOUT THE AUTHOR

ANNA KATMORE prefers blue to green, spring to winter, and writing to almost everything else. It helps her escape from a boring world to something with actual adventure and romance, she says. Even when she's not crafting a new story, you'll see her lounging with a book in some quiet spot. She was 17 when she left Vienna to live in the tranquil countryside of Austria, and from there she loves to plan trips with her family to anywhere in the world. Two of her favorite places? Disneyland and the deep dungeons of her creative mind.

For more information, please visit her website at www.annakatmore.com

14455548R00176

Printed in Great Britain
by Amazon.co.uk, Ltd.,
Marston Gate.